"I want you, Paige," Kellen said, his voice husky.

"But I can't read your mind. Whatever you decide will be the way it will go. I told you once I'd never take anything from you that you weren't prepared to give. I meant that."

She wanted him so much, Paige thought. Now. This minute. She had said these hours would be theirs. Yet. . . . What would become of her if she gave herself totally to this man? She had enjoyed every moment of their time together, but if she passed into his care the very essence of her being would be lost. Kellen had invoked passions within her she did not know she possessed. Oh, Lord, what if she came to love him? He might never love her in return and . . . "Kellen, I . . ." she said. "I can't. Not . . . yet."

He smiled and kissed her quickly. "Enough said."

"You must think I'm a tease, a—"

"You are, Paige Cunningham, the one who makes me laugh right out loud. You are the one who makes me so angry I could paddle that cute little tush of yours. You are the one who makes me forget the madness I work in and remember who I am. You are . . . my lady."

For how long? she thought, shivering slightly. Oh, Kellen, for how long?

Bantam Books by Joan Elliott Pickart
Ask your bookseller for the titles you have missed

BREAKING ALL THE RULES
(*Loveswept #61*)

CHARADE
(*Loveswept #74*)

WHAT ARE *LOVESWEPT* ROMANCES?

They are stories of true romance and touching emotion. We believe those two very important ingredients are constants in our highly sensual and very believable stories in the *LOVESWEPT* line. Our goal is to give you, the reader, stories of consistently high quality that may sometimes make you laugh, sometimes make you cry, but are always fresh and creative and contain many delightful surprises within their pages.

Most romance fans read an enormous number of books. Those they truly love, they keep. Others may be traded with friends and soon forgotten. We hope that each *LOVESWEPT* romance will be a treasure—a "keeper." We will always try to publish

LOVE STORIES YOU'LL NEVER FORGET
BY AUTHORS YOU'LL ALWAYS REMEMBER

The Editors

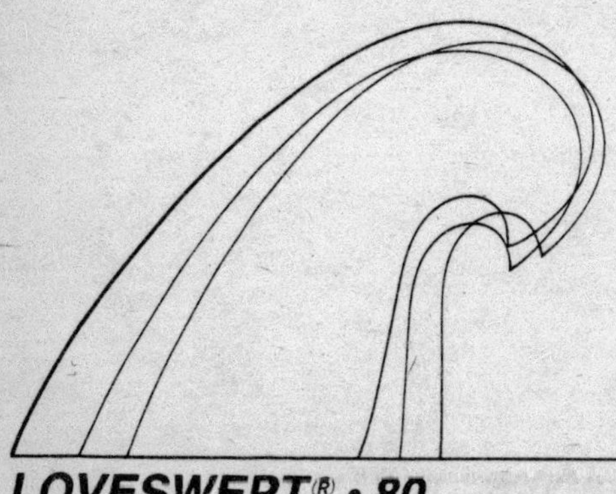

LOVESWEPT® • 80

Joan Elliott Pickart

The Finishing Touch

BANTAM BOOKS
TORONTO • NEW YORK • LONDON • SYDNEY • AUCKLAND

THE FINISHING TOUCH
A Bantam Book / February 1985

LOVESWEPT® and the wave device are registered trademarks of Bantam Books, Inc. Registered in U.S. Patent and Trademark Office and elsewhere.

ISBN 0-553-21691-0

Published simultaneously in the United States and Canada

Bantam Books are published by Bantam Books, Inc. Its trademark, consisting of the words "Bantam Books" and the portrayal of a rooster, is Registered in U.S. Patent and Trademark Office and in other countries. Marca Registrada. Bantam Books, Inc., 666 Fifth Avenue, New York, New York 10103.

PRINTED IN THE UNITED STATES OF AMERICA

O 0 9 8 7 6 5 4 3 2 1

For my mother and mother-in-law,
with love and gratitude

One

Paige Cunningham hugged her arms tightly around herself as she viewed the scene below her. From her vantage point seven floors above Central Avenue, she could watch as the traffic surged up and down the busy Phoenix street. Her large dark brown eyes swept over the gold, red, and green Christmas decorations that were hanging from the multitude of light poles, and the properly suited Santa Claus standing on the corner, dutifully waving his bell in a steady rhythm.

In spite of the warmth in the plush office, Paige shivered as an icy chill washed over her, accompanied by a wave of haunting memories. Taking a deep breath, she turned from the window, walked to her desk, and sat down in the leather chair. She leaned back and closed her eyes, forcing herself to relax and trying to push the distressing thoughts from her mind.

Christmas, she thought. In three weeks it would be upon her again with its ghosts and torment and—

"Mrs. Cunningham?" a voice said, interrupting Paige's reverie. "Oh, excuse me, I didn't realize you were resting."

"I wasn't," Paige said, sitting up and forcing a smile. "Just thinking. Was there something you needed, Janet?"

"I was . . . well, I mean . . . is it true?"

"Is what true?"

"Are you really going to decorate a house for Kellen Davis, the movie star?"

"News travels fast." Paige laughed softly. "Actually, Janet, nothing is definite. We received a call from Mr. Davis's representative asking this firm to present our ideas and cost projection. We'll be one of several bidding, I imagine."

"But just think of it," Janet rushed on. "You'll be meeting Kellen Davis! Oh, I would die. I would! Did you see him in *Master's Touch*? He was so sexy, I could hardly stand it! I swear he had his shirt off more than it was on, and that body is unbelievable! He—"

"Janet," Paige interrupted, "Mr. Davis won't be at the house when I view it this afternoon."

"Why not?" the girl asked, a look of utter disappointment on her face.

"He's busy working on location here for his new picture. I'm meeting with a Mr. Winslow. Do you think you can calm down long enough to go answer the phone?"

"Oh, gosh, I didn't even hear it." Janet dashed from the room.

Paige smiled and shook her head. Janet certainly was a loyal fan of Kellen Davis's. Paige had not admitted to the young girl that she, too, had seen *Master's Touch* and, yes, Kellen Davis was a gorgeous hunk of man. Paige was relieved he wouldn't be at the house while she was there. She could do without dealing with an egotistical superstar who was probably so full of his own importance, he wouldn't listen to a word she said. She hoped this Mr. Winslow was a reasonable person.

"Paige, are you all set to win the hearts and wallets of the Hollywood set?" a man said, coming into the office.

"Hello, Paul," Paige said, smiling warmly. "I'm as ready as I can be, I guess."

"Don't let them talk you into taking a screen test, my beauty. I can't afford to lose you."

"Paul, I swear you need glasses." Paige laughed. "You look chilled. May I pour you a cup of coffee?"

He nodded. "Sounds good. Phoenix may seem like Paradise to the snowbirds who flock here for the winter, but it's darn chilly out there."

Paige rose from behind the desk and walked to the far end of the spacious room. She was aware of, but not offended by, Paul's admiring look. She knew her pale blue wool dress fitted her well, draping softly over her slender hips and lovingly molding to her full breasts. And she was proud of her shapely legs, which were accentuated by her high-heeled black pumps. She walked back to Paul and handed him a cup of steaming coffee.

"Thank you," he said, looking at her thoughtfully over the rim as he sipped the liquid.

"Paul?"

"What? Oh, sorry, Paige, I was defrosting my brain." He sat down in one of the chairs that faced Paige's desk. "You bundle up when you go out. It's really nasty out there."

"Yes, sir," she said, leaning back against her desk, "but my arithmetic says you're not old enough to be my father."

"Oh, I don't know about that." He chuckled. "I'm

forty and you're twenty-seven. I was a fast-maturing kid."

"I bet you were. By the way, how is your lovely Elda?"

"I'm not seeing her anymore," he said, staring into his cup.

"Paul Martin! You are unbelievable." Paige frowned and folded her arms across her breasts. "What happened this time?"

"She wore me out," he said gloomily. "That girl was really into the nightlife. Party, party, party, that's all we did. She never heard of a quiet evening at home. I'm too ancient for that stuff."

"Well, you'll replace her soon enough."

"Lord, Paige, you make me sound like a playboy. That's not a very respectful way to talk about your boss."

"I'm sorry, but you must admit that in the year and a half I've been here, I've needed a scorecard to keep track of your ladies, you handsome devil."

"I'm . . . avoiding another commitment," he said, shifting uncomfortably in his chair.

"Oh, Paul," Paige said, her voice softening, "we've had this discussion before. Just because you had a disastrous marriage doesn't mean—"

"Look who's talking," he said. "I don't see you hurrying down the aisle. You keep men at arm's length. You've built walls around yourself that—"

"Don't, Paul," she said quietly. "My circumstances are different and you know it."

"Why?" he asked, getting to his feet and setting the cup on the desk before beginning to pace the floor. "Because you're a widow? You're still alone, Paige. You seem to think that's a life sentence."

"I'm doing just fine, thank you," she snapped.

Paul walked to the windows and stared down at the bustling scene below. Paige watched as he ran his hand over the back of his neck in a gesture of frustration. Paul Martin appeared younger than his forty years, his blond hair and blue eyes giving him an almost boyish quality. He was approximately five feet ten with a trim, well-proportioned body that was flatteringly outlined in the perfectly cut three-piece suit he was wearing. He had married his college sweetheart and their divorce nearly three years before had shattered him. Intelligent, charming, and wealthy, he was constantly sought after by the high society ladies of Phoenix and, with the multitude of available women, spent his time flitting between affairs.

While Paige did not quite approve of Paul's lifestyle, she judged him only for the man he was in relationship to herself. He was her employer, the owner of the House of Martin, one of the most elite interior decorating firms in Phoenix, but more than that, he was her friend. They often enjoyed a late dinner together after working past regular hours and felt at ease in each other's company. On many occasions Paul had poured out his dissatisfactions regarding his most recent companion and Paige would listen with a sympathetic ear. Now she was staring at him sternly until he dropped his gaze to the floor.

"Okay," he said, throwing up his hands. "I'm sorry. I'm out of line again. It's just that . . . well, I worry about you."

"I know," she said, "but you shouldn't. I'm a big girl now and perfectly capable of taking care of myself. I appreciate your concern, Paul, I really do. I consider you my dear friend and I cherish that. Now, I've got to be on my way to the great Kellen Davis's abode. And yes, I'll button up my coat."

"Knock 'em dead," Paul said with a smile.

"Do my best, Coach." She waved, picked up her purse, coat, and briefcase, and walked to the door. "I'll report in later."

"Remember, no screen tests," he called after her, and smiled again as her lilting laughter reached his ears.

As Paige maneuvered her compact car through the traffic her thoughts lingered on Paul Martin. Dear Paul. He had been through another disastrous affair. It was as though he purposely picked women who were wrong for him, Paige mused. But was that really so hard to understand? She dated only men who were safe, wanted no more than a pleasant evening and a casual good-night kiss at her door. Paul and Paige, she thought. Two misfits. They sounded like a vaudeville team. Oh, wonderful! It was starting to rain.

Within minutes heavy sheets of water were spilling onto the windshield, and Paige slowed her speed, leaning forward to afford a better view as the wipers struggled under the torrent. Her progress was slow as she made her way through the intriguing town of Scottsdale. The entire main street of the city depicted the Old West, each storefront boasting rustic wood with hitching posts that lined the edges of the sidewalks. Paige enjoyed shopping in the pleasant atmosphere, wandering for hours through the endless small shops. Fifth Avenue was a cluster of fashionable boutiques, and Paige often selected her clothes from the marvelous variety available there.

She quickly tugged a piece of paper from her purse and stole a glance at it while trying to keep an eye on the milling traffic. She knew she was headed for an area behind the renowned Camelback Mountain, but the directions to Kellen Davis's house would weave her through the intricate roads of the foothills. It was a location reserved for the elite, the very wealthy, and while she had once decorated a home for a prestigious resident there, she knew no one personally who could afford such a luxurious life-style. Passing the famous mountain, she was unable to decipher its remarkable shape in the driving rain, but knew it truly did resemble a resting camel and was worthy of its reputation as a phenomenon of nature.

Barely moving along the water-drenched roads, Paige peered out the window, trying to read the street signs as they came into view. She drove farther off the main thoroughfare, encountering bumpy narrow paths that twisted and turned. The driving rain was chewing holes in the previously dry soil.

"Thank goodness," she sighed, at last seeing the street she was looking for. "Kellen Davis won't have to worry about his fans storming the gates of his castle. They'll never find it!"

She raised her brows and nodded in approval as the enormous structure came into view. Even with the inclement weather she could see the red-tile roof atop the two-story house. The outer walls were stark white, giving an overall impression of a Spanish hacienda. Wrought-iron balconies, which, Paige assumed, led off just a few of many second-floor bedrooms, wrapped around tall double doors. A circular driveway curved in front of the majestic home, and she parked as close as possible to the wide steps that led to hand-carved doors across a large expanse of porch.

Grateful that she had tossed her umbrella in the backseat that morning when the weather had appeared threatening, she snatched it up and, after organizing her purse and briefcase, opened the car door, popped open the flowered protector, and dashed up the slippery stairs. A heavy brass door knocker resounded noisily when she rapped it against its base, and the wooden panel swung open almost immediately.

"Come in. Come in," a small, plump man appearing to be in his fifties said. "Get out of that nasty rain."

"Thank you," Paige said, stepping into the entryway. "Perhaps I should leave my umbrella outside so it doesn't drip on the floor."

"Nonsense. Just drop it right there. Am I correct in assuming you are Mrs. Cunningham from the House of Martin?"

"You are." She smiled.

"I'm Timmy Winslow."

"I'm pleased to meet you, Mr. Winslow."

"May I get you a drink to take off the chill? We're short on furniture around here, but the bar is well stocked."

"No, thank you. I'm fine."

"Well, give me your coat and then I'll show you the living room, such as it is."

Her umbrella dripped steadily on the Spanish-tile floor; her coat lay draped over a lawn chair. Paige followed Timmy Winslow across the hall and into an enormous room that boasted thick-pile burnt orange carpeting. A massive stone fireplace in the far wall beckoned with a roaring fire. Narrow floor-to-ceiling bookshelves were on either side of the hearth. Several cushioned lounge chairs sat close to the fireplace, the bright plastic furniture obviously belonging in a backyard or surrounding a swimming pool. The lawn ensemble was the only addition to the room, and Paige had the disquieting thought that her voice would echo if she spoke aloud.

"We should rent it out as a dance hall," Timmy Winslow said with a chuckle. "Properly decorated, it will be a splendid area, but at the moment it's a disaster. Can you believe that wallpaper? Flocked pea soup. It's awful. It's got to go."

"That's a relief." Paige laughed, warming to the personality of the smartly dressed man. "It would be rather difficult to work around. Perhaps you could give me some idea as to how Mr. Davis plans to furnish his home."

"Well, Kellen is a big man and needs sofas and chairs appropriate to his size. He wants this room done in a combination of Spanish and western motifs, and he prefers warm colors, earth tones."

"I see." She retrieved a pad and pen from her briefcase and jotted this down.

Suddenly the front door was slammed with such force that both Paige and Timmy looked up in startled surprise. Heavy footsteps could be heard approaching across the entryway and within moments a tall, broad-shouldered, glowering man clad in dark slacks and a sheepskin jacket strode into the room.

"Kellen," Timmy said, "whatever are you doing here? I thought you—"

"We got rained out. I'm wet, cold, and so hungry, I think I'm going to pass out. This has not been a terrific day."

Sweet heaven, Paige thought, he was . . . he was gorgeous! So this was the great Kellen Davis. He was even better-looking than he appeared in the movies, and taller. He had to be six feet four. And those shoulders! Thick black hair, a deep tan, and—if he ever realized she was in the room and looked at her—she'd see if his eyes were as blue as they appeared on the silver screen. Oh, no, he was taking off his coat. He was getting better by the minute. The black turtleneck sweater was an excellent choice, but she was sure he was perfectly aware of that.

"Have a drink, Kellen," Timmy said, "and warm up your bones. By the way, this is Mrs. Cunningham, the decorator from the House of Martin."

"Mrs. Cunningham." Kellen nodded, glanced at Paige, then scrutinized her more carefully as he took in her slender figure silhouetted against the roaring fire. She was lovely, Kellen thought suddenly. Her thick, almost black hair was pulled straight back from her face and coiled into a chignon at the nape of her neck. She looked regal; her high cheekbones and huge dark eyes were classic and complemented her delicate mouth and soft-appearing lips marvelously. She was, he guessed, maybe five feet six in her stocking feet and had an air of fragility about her. But it was her eyes that fascinated him. She reminded him of a fawn, a graceful deer.

"Mr. Davis," Paige said, returning his steady gaze. Blue as sapphires, she thought, looking directly into the deep pools of his eyes. She had never met such a masculine man. It sounded dumb, but there was a sense of power, of virility about him. It wasn't just his size; it was something else, an underlying authority, a—

"Kellen?" Timmy said, looking at the man, who had not moved or spoken since addressing Paige.

"What? Oh, yes, Timmy," Kellen said, redirecting his attention to Timmy Winslow. "I'm going to change into dry clothes. You'll excuse me, Mrs. Cunningham?"

"Yes, of course," she said, nodding slightly.

Paige watched as Kellen Davis moved in long strides across the room and bounded up the stairs two at a time. He reminded her of a panther. Strong, sleek, and probably equally as dangerous.

"Time out," Timmy said cheerfully. "When Kellen says he's hungry, he isn't kidding. I'd better haul some food out before he starts chewing on a chair. We don't have enough of those to go around as it is. Follow me, my dear, we're off to the kitchen."

"Whatever," Paige muttered, dropping her pad and pen into the open briefcase on the floor and following Timmy out of the room.

The kitchen was large and bright and had been done in varying shades of yellow. A butcher-block counter stood in the middle of the room while spotless stainless-steel appliances sat against the walls. The cupboards were constructed of dark wood, the front of each appearing to have been handcarved with intricate scrollwork. The only blemish in the area was a rickety picnic table liberally spotted with paint and two benches in similar condition.

"Love the table," Paige said, laughing softly.

"We found it in the backyard with the lawn furniture. Classy, huh? Oh, well, beats eating standing up. I think you can see, Mrs. Cunningham, how desperately Kellen needs your services."

"Yes." She smiled. "I'd say you have a bit of an emergency situation here."

"Not me," Timmy said, opening the refrigerator, pulling out dishes, and placing them on the table. "I don't live in this monastery. This is Kellen's baby. I'm nicely stowed away at the Camelback Inn, and I'm very comfortable. You wouldn't catch me roughing it here. Kellen doesn't even have a bed yet. The dopy guy is camped out upstairs in a sleeping bag."

"Why doesn't he go to a hotel until the house is ready to be occupied?"

"He's sick of 'em. He bought this house, and he's determined to live in it while we're here shooting the picture. Besides, he has problems with privacy in hotels. He can't walk across the lobby without people flocking around him. He made up his mind that things would be different this time. And believe me, my dear, once Kellen Davis decides on something, that's the way it's going to be. There! That ought to hold him until dinner."

"There's enough food there for an army," Paige said.

"He's a big man with an appetite to match," Timmy said. "Why don't you grab a plate and help yourself?"

"No, thank you. I had lunch just before I came."

"Are you trying to ruin Mrs. Cunningham's lovely

figure, Timmy?" Kellen asked, coming up behind them.

"Nope, just being a model host," Timmy said. "Sit down and eat, Kellen."

Paige glanced quickly at Kellen Davis, her gaze lingering long enough to take in his muscular frame outlined in tight-fitting faded jeans and a green V-neck sweater. Black curly hair crept above the neckline of the sweater, which clung to his broad chest and pulled against his flat stomach. The rich color accentuated Kellen's dark good looks, and white teeth flashed as he smiled at the offering before him.

"Please join me, Mrs. Cunningham," he said, looking up at Paige. "You, too, Timmy. Even if you're not hungry, you can give me your ideas on the house while I feed myself."

She wasn't wearing a wedding ring, Kellen thought, observing Paige's hand where she rested it on the table after sitting down opposite him. Maybe she was one of those liberated types who didn't like the symbol of bondage. No, he didn't think so. If that was true, she'd probably use *Ms.* instead of *Mrs.* So, Mrs. Cunningham, with the enchanting big brown eyes, where was Mr. Cunningham? Personally he hoped he was on a slow boat to China. My Lord, she was so damn attractive. No—more. She was intriguing.

"Have you lived in Phoenix long?" he asked Paige as he filled his plate with food.

"About a year and a half," she said, her eyes widening slightly at the proportions he was serving himself.

"Oh? Where did you move from?"

"Colorado."

"That's quite a switch of climates. What made you choose Phoenix? Did your husband's work bring you here?"

"No."

"Oh," he said, shoveling a forkful of food into his mouth. Well, damn, he thought. That hadn't gone so hot. Maybe he should quit playing games and just ask her. "Are you married?" he said, looking at her once again.

"I'm a widow, Mr. Davis," she said, her jaw tightening slightly.

"I'm sorry."

"So am I."

Kellen fumed at himself: he'd blown it. He had just barged in and opened his big mouth. He had seen it, the raw pain flashing through her eyes. She made a man want to pull her close, protect her from— What was the matter with him? He didn't even know this woman!

"I believe you wanted to hear my ideas for the decorating of your home, Mr. Davis," Paige said with a sudden coolness. "I'm afraid all I've seen so far is the living room and—"

"That's fine." Kellen nodded. "Did you explain the problem, Timmy?"

"No, I hadn't gotten that far," the older man said. "There's the phone ringing. I'll get it."

"Problem, Mr. Davis?" Paige said.

"Look, call me Kellen and I'll call you . . . Now, there's the mystery. I don't know your first name," he said, flashing her a dazzling smile.

He should do toothpaste commercials, she thought, suppressing a laugh that threatened to erupt. "Paige," she said, the swallowed giggle showing itself in the form of a warm smile.

"Don't ever play poker, Paige," he said quietly.

"Pardon me?"

"Your eyes reflect your feelings like neon signs. You really do have the most remarkable eyes."

She couldn't believe he had said that, and she

shook her head slightly. Which one of his movies had he borrowed that line from? He looked sincere but, after all, the man was an actor. He probably had hustling down to an art. "Thank you," she said, "but they came with my face. I really didn't have anything to do with it."

Kellen looked at her in surprise and then put his head back and roared with laughter. The sound was rich and throaty, and Paige found herself smiling, although she had absolutely no idea what was so funny.

"You think I'm trying to do a number on you, don't you?" he said when he finally caught his breath. "I don't blame you. I guess it sounded pretty corny."

"Well, I—"

"I meant it though," he continued, his expression now serious. "Paige Cunningham, you have the loveliest eyes I've seen since I can remember, and that's the truth. For some unexplainable reason I hope you believe me when I say that."

"All right, Kellen, then I'll graciously accept your compliment. Now, suppose we get back to this problem of yours."

So much for that, he thought, taking a bite of cheese. She was a cool cookie. He should jump up on the table and yell, "Woman, I am Kellen Davis, the sex symbol of America. It is time for you to throw yourself at my feet like the rest of your fair sex." Why did he get the feeling she was very unimpressed with who and what he was? Interesting lady. Ah! There was an important clue! She was a real lady. It had been a helluva long time since he'd crossed paths with one of those.

"Mr. Davis?"

"Huh? Oh, hey, it's Kellen, remember?"

"All right . . . Kellen. Could we—"

"Kellen," Timmy said, bustling back into the room,

"that was Art on the phone. There's a mixup on some of the equipment, and I said I'd drive in and help sort things out."

"Sure, Timmy, go ahead," Kellen said. "No need to come back out later unless there's something we have to go over."

"Okay. Nice to have met you, Mrs. Cunningham." Timmy smiled at her. "Oh, Kellen, the other two decorating firms said they'd have cost figures for you by tomorrow afternoon."

"Fine." Kellen nodded, redirecting his attention to the food on his plate.

"Bye, y'all." Timmy waved and hurried from the room.

I, Paige Cunningham, am absolutely, totally, completely alone with Kellen Davis, the world-famous movie star, Paige thought wildly. Calm down. Don't panic. He was a mere man. He put his pants on one leg—Lord, don't start thinking about him with his pants off! She was acting so silly. They'd discuss her decorating ideas and then she'd trot herself back to the office. That would be that.

"I think I'll live," Kellen said, pushing the empty plate away. "Man, I was starving. Now, let me tell you my tale of woe while I put this stuff back in the refrigerator."

The great Kellen Davis cleaned up his own messes? Paige thought, smiling as he got up from the table and began to put away the dishes of food.

"You see," he said, continuing with his chore, "I promised the crew from the movie a fabulous Christmas party and I'll be darned if I'll have it in a hotel. I want it here, in this house. Some of them have families and are going home for the holidays, so I planned it for the night before Christmas Eve. But," he finished, sitting back down at the now empty table, "I can't very well entertain with no furniture to sit on. Right?"

"But . . . my gosh, no one could get a house this size completely decorated in only three weeks!"

"I know, I know," he said quickly. "All I'd need done is the living room. Oh, and a decent table out here for the caterers to use. That's not too much to ask, is it?"

"Well, the wallpaper has to be stripped and everything painted. Do you like the carpeting? It would help if you did. You'd have to pick stock furniture, nothing custom-made, of course."

"Then you'll do it, Paige?"

"Me? You haven't reviewed the suggestions from the other—"

"I don't intend to," he said quietly, looking directly into her eyes. "I've made my decision. I've chosen you for the job."

"I— Thank you," she said, unable to tear her gaze from his compelling blue eyes.

Neither moved nor spoke; the only sound in the room was the noise of the rain beating against the windows. Paige felt mesmerized, held tightly in place, hardly able to breathe as time stood still. A slight frown crossed Kellen's handsome features and, as if coming out of a trance, he stood up abruptly and cleared his throat.

"Why don't we go back into the living room," he said, his voice strangely husky, "and you can toss some of your ideas out for discussion?"

"Fine," Paige said, acutely aware that her knees were trembling slightly as she rose to join him. What had happened? she thought. Everything seemed to have stopped. He had looked at her so intensely and she had felt . . . what? It was so strange, so . . . She had to keep away from this man. He had a magnetism, an unnatural pull on her senses. She didn't like it. No, not one little bit.

Kellen stepped back and allowed Paige to move ahead of him out of the kitchen. She was a witch, he thought, shaking his head. She'd cast him under some kind of weird spell for a moment there. All he had wanted to do was stare at that lovely face and etch it indelibly in his mind. This was ridiculous! Sure, she was pretty, but so were plenty of others. She wasn't that special. Was she? There was just something about her that—

"Bookshelves," Paige said, staring at the empty expanses on each side of the fireplace.

"You're absolutely right." Kellen nodded, grinning down at her.

"They mean trouble."

"Why?"

"Because no matter how much we put in the room, unless those shelves are relatively full, the room will have the appearance of not being completed."

"Oh."

"We can use some knickknacks but we've got to have books too. I—" Paige started, only to suddenly burst into laughter.

"What's wrong?" he asked, smiling, delighted at the infectious sound.

"I was remembering an apartment I did for a woman over in Mesa. She had shelves but would allow only books with blue covers."

"You're kidding."

"No, I'm serious. She didn't care who the authors were—and she had no intention of reading any of the books—but she simply demanded they be blue! Paul and I must have gone to fifty stores buying every—"

"Paul?"

"My boss, Paul Martin. He owns the House of Martin. Anyway, every time I recall that and— Goodness, I hope you have some favorite titles so I won't be shopping for *blue*."

"You mean I can't have all purple dustcovers? Darn it, Paige, I'm really disappointed."

"I don't think I should have told you about the woman in Mesa."

"How did her place look when you finished?"

"Actually it was quite nice. The solid wall of blue books was rather unique. You know, Kellen, I was assuming we'd have to purchase all these things, but surely you own another home. Maybe you'd prefer to have some of your belongings shipped here."

"No," he said, shoving his hands into his pockets and frowning, "there's nothing. My house in Beverly Hills burned to the ground several months ago."

"Oh, my! I'm so sorry. That must have been a terrible experience. Did you lose everything? All your mementos and—"

"Yes."

"Oh, Kellen," she said softly, reaching out and placing her hand on his arm.

Again their eyes met. Again the almost eerie silence fell over them. Again there was no time or space or reality within the long moment that held them immobile. Unconsciously Kellen covered Paige's delicate hand with his large one. She could feel the warmth of his touch spreading throughout her as a strange tingling sensation started somewhere deep within her and danced across her senses. In the farthest regions of her mind she registered that the look in Kellen's eyes was changing. The sapphire-blue pools were now slightly cloudy, and she saw desire there. His fingertips tightened on hers, but she did not pull her hand away as she gazed up at him.

He wanted to kiss her, Kellen realized. No, far more than that. He could imagine making love to this beautiful creature, seeing passion in those enormous brown eyes. Dammit, Davis, back off. He'd frighten her away. She was like a skittish colt. If he even looked at her wrong, she was liable to cut and run. He didn't want that to happen. He had no idea why it mattered so much but . . . "I felt bad about the house at first," he said suddenly, causing Paige to drop her hand from his arm, "but then I realized it was only material things. I might have died in that fire if I had been home, and I'm glad I'm alive. There are certain items I'll never be able to replace that were special only to me, but I have them stored in my mind."

"I'm not sure I could be so brave about the whole thing," Paige said.

"I think you realize the inner strengths people draw on when disaster strikes, Paige. You're awfully young to be a widow, which means your life has not been all sunshine and laughter. You've shed tears, more than probably seems fair. But you also must know about cherishing the memories. Nothing can ever rob you of those."

Sudden, unexpected tears sprang to Paige's eyes, and she turned in embarrassment, walking to the fireplace where she stared into the flames. Kellen's strong hands gripped her shoulders and pulled her around to within inches of his massive chest.

"I'm sorry if I upset you," he said softly.

"No, no, you didn't. I—"

Oh, God, he thought, his willpower had just run out. It was the tears. She looked so sad, so incredibly sad. "Oh, Paige, don't cry," he whispered as he lowered his lips to hers. "Please, don't cry."

The kiss was soft and warm and tender, and Paige shut her eyes and received the lips that claimed hers. She hesitated only a fraction of a second before meeting Kellen's tongue as it gently sought the dark regions of her mouth. He slowly gathered her to him, pressing her breasts against his rock-hard chest as her arms reached up to encircle his neck.

The kiss intensified. The tempo quickened as he

pulled her closer, running his hands down her slender back. She returned his ardor feverishly, molding against him, sinking her fingertips into his thick dark hair. Reason was gone. Reality was gone. There was only now, this moment in time as Paige felt an inner stirring of desire start to glow. Long-forgotten wants and needs burst into leaping flames that threatened to consume her. She heard a soft moan and knew it had come from herself as their breathing became raspy and labored. She could feel the evidence of Kellen's arousal pressing against her and irrationally marveled that she had excited this epitome of virility.

Her mind screamed for her to stop, to regain her composure and control, to tear herself from this man's grasp and flee. But she didn't want to. It had been so long, so very long since she had felt feminine and alive. Kellen's mouth and arms and body were holding her fast, and she drank in the feel and aroma of his massive frame. She wasn't alone anymore. She was wrapped in overpowering strength, drowning in the sensations that were sweeping through her.

"Paige," he murmured, his lips traveling down the slender column of her neck. "Oh, Paige."

The sound of her name caused her to stiffen and gasp. Her eyes widened in horror. "My God," she said, pulling out of his reach, "what am I doing?"

"Paige . . ." He moved toward her.

"No! Don't! I can't believe this happened!"

"It wasn't wrong, Paige," he said softly. "We responded to each other. We shared something special. You can't deny that you liked what you were experiencing. Your body was answering mine. We were—"

"Indulging in old-fashioned lust," she snapped, folding her arms protectively over her breasts.

"Is that what you really think?" he asked, his jaw tightening slightly.

"What else could it be? We don't even know each other! I realize I've given you a false picture of myself. I don't usually go leaping into the arms of my clients. I hope you're enough of a gentleman to forget this ever took place."

"I can't do that," he said, shoving his hands into his pockets and smiling at her. "Kissing you, holding you, has now become one of those memories I told you I've learned to store away. You can dismiss your part in it from your mind if you want to, but I'm not. I'm keeping my half."

"I think you're a little bit crazy," Paige said, smiling in spite of herself.

"It helps in this business I'm in. Onward and upward, Mrs. Cunningham. What kind of couch do I get for this room?"

"Sofa, Mr. Davis," she said, relieved the tension had lifted. "Decorators always call them sofas."

"Whatever." He shrugged. Thank heavens, she hadn't torn out of the house, he thought as he absently listened to her suggestions for the groupings and helped her measure the length and width of the room. He shouldn't have touched her. But, oh, Lord, she had felt so good in his arms! She was protecting herself, he could tell, but he had had a glimpse of the real Paige Cunningham. She was warm and giving, and capable of making love with total abandonment. He had lost control of himself. It was as if she had pushed a button and he was a goner. He couldn't allow that to happen twice. He'd smoothed it over this time, but he'd bet she wouldn't forgive him again. He'd have to move slowly or— Why was he worried about it? He didn't have to set up a complicated campaign to get a woman into his bed. There were plenty out there who would jump at the chance. Was it because she was a challenge? Was that what had him going? Hell, he didn't know!

". . . and another smaller cluster of chairs in that area," Paige said.

"Huh? Oh, yes, great." He nodded.

"Kellen, have you heard one word of this?" she asked.

"I'm sorry, Paige. I was in a different time zone for a minute there. Why don't you draw me a picture or something and show it to me tomorrow?"

"Well, all right, if that's what you prefer."

"Listen, would you come up to my bedroom?"

"I beg your pardon?" she said, her eyes wide.

"What I mean is," he said quickly, "I need your advice. I've been sleeping on the floor for a week since I got here and this camping-out number is getting stale. I thought if you saw the size of the room, you'd know what I should have."

"Oh."

"A king-size bed is a must," he added, moving toward the stairs, "or my feet hang over the end. Other than that, I'll leave it up to you."

"Okay." She joined him and walked next to him up the stairs. She *would* forget what had happened, she told herself. Wouldn't she? He could do whatever he pleased with his half of that disastrous event, but she was erasing it from her mind. She had gotten caught up in his status, his movie-star mystique, that was all. It meant nothing. Her behavior was inexcusable. She'd never before responded to a man's kiss like that! She should be thankful she'd gotten out of the situation so easily. He could have gotten angry because she had led him on. She had not. Yes, she had. But his lips were so warm, enticing, and she just—

"Here it is," Kellen said, pushing open a door at the

end of a long corridor. "Can you get me a bed by tomorrow?"

"Tomorrow!"

"My poor back can't take much more of this. Please?" he begged, grinning engagingly.

"I suppose I can, but it will cost more for a special delivery out here."

"I don't care. Just think, only one painful night in misery remains and then I'll have a real honest-to-goodness bed. That will call for a celebration."

"I still think you should move to a hotel for a while. I'm going to have to bring workmen in here to paint the living room. It's going to be a mess."

"Nope. Once I make up my mind about something, I'm very stubborn."

Paige laughed. "I'll keep that information handy. It might keep us from crossing swords."

"Oh, I don't anticipate us having any problems getting along," he said pleasantly. "Our relationship simply calls for some give and take."

"Our what?"

"You know," he said, turning and walking from the room, "you're the decorator and I'm the client."

"Oh, yes, of course," she said, staring after him for a moment before following him down the corridor.

Two

Downstairs in the living room Paige snapped her briefcase shut and turned to face Kellen. "If I can arrange delivery of your bed for tomorrow, will Mr. Winslow be here?"

"Not necessarily," Kellen said. "Timmy could be anywhere at any time. I'll give you my spare key and you can let yourself in." He handed her a key.

"All right," she said. "May I keep this for a while? It will make it easier once I contract with the painters and other delivery people."

"Sure."

"I'll do a sketch of this room tonight and leave it here when I come with the furniture men."

"Bad plan," he said, shaking his head.

"Why?"

"Because it wastes time. I won't see the drawing until tomorrow night. Then we'll have to set up a time for the next day to hash it over."

"Well . . ."

"I'll tell you what, Paige. I'll come by your place after we finish on location, preview the ideas you have, and take you out to dinner."

"Out to— I really don't think—"

"We both have to eat," he said, flashing her a marvelous smile. "What's your address?"

Paige had repeated the number of her apartment building before she was totally aware she had even opened her mouth.

"I should be there by seven," he said. "I'll call you if I get tied up. Are you in the phone book?"

"Yes. Now, I must be getting back to the office. Paul will be wondering where I am."

"Ah, yes, Paul." Kellen nodded. "He must have been around for a long time. The House of Martin has a reputation one doesn't build overnight."

"If you're implying that he's tottering on his last legs, he's not." She smiled. "Being forty doesn't make him eligible for the old folks' home. He's a very talented man who works hard at his craft. He's earned the respect his firm has gained."

"You sound very fond of him," Kellen said, frowning slightly.

"We're close friends. I must go. Good-bye, Kellen, it was . . . a pleasure."

"I'll see you to the door."

In the entryway Paige closed the now dry umbrella and picked up her coat, which Kellen took from her and held out for her. His fingers lingered on her shoulders after she had shrugged into the coat, and she made a pretense of busily picking up her belongings before looking at him again.

"Until tomorrow night," he said quietly, looking directly into her large eyes.

"Fine. Good-bye," she said, and hurried out the door, nearly running down the front steps to her car.

"Good-bye, pretty Paige," Kellen said softly, closing the door behind her.

The rain had stopped, but the sky was heavy with ominous dark clouds as Paige drove back to the city, her hands tightly gripping the steering wheel. She felt as though she had been to a faraway land, another planet even, and had now returned. In a way it was true. Kellen Davis was from a different world. He was a Hollywood star, accustomed to a glamorous life with its money and . . . fast women? Was that how he had seen her? If he had, it was her own fault, she decided miserably. He had touched her and she'd practically crawled inside his shirt! She could only hope she had made it perfectly clear that she usually didn't behave in such a manner. Lord, that sounded pompous, Paige told herself. But it was true. She would put the whole incident out of her mind. It had certainly meant nothing to Kellen. A man like that went around snapping his fingers and watching the women jump into his bed. He had said it himself: he was the client, she was the decorator. Pure and simple. *That* took care of *that*, thank you very much!

Janet had her nose buried in a magazine when Paige entered the office and was totally unaware that her boss had returned.

"Hello?" Paige asked, jiggling the girl's arm. "Are you in there?"

"Oh! Mrs. Cunningham! I'm sorry."

Paige smiled. "What are you reading that had you so deeply engrossed?"

"I went out on my lunch hour and bought this movie magazine with an article on Kellen Davis. See? Here's his picture. No shirt. Isn't he gorgeous? There's a rumor that he had an affair with Hildy Holt while they were filming *Master's Touch*. She's so beautiful. But then it says she flounced off to Paris because he chose Felicia Evans to star with him in

Love Me Less. That's the one he's making here right now. Anyway, according to this—"

"Janet," Paige interrupted, "that's all very interesting, but do you know if Mr. Martin is in?"

"I think so. What did Kellen Davis's house look like? Was it awesome?"

"It's very big and very empty," Paige said over her shoulder as she walked away. Until Kellen walked in the room, she thought. That aura of power he possessed seemed to fill even the largest expanse. He was intimidating. He also oozed masculinity, and she was not getting within ten feet of him again!

"Paige, come in," Paul said when she poked her head in his office doorway. "How did it go?"

"We got a slice of the pie," she said, sinking wearily onto the chair in front of his desk. "Master bedroom to be done tomorrow. Living room and kitchen table by Christmas."

"Is there a reason for this unusual timetable?"

"He's sleeping on the floor and having a party the night before Christmas Eve."

"The jet set is strange," Paul said, shaking his head. "But congratulations on getting that much. What's the deal on the rest of the house?"

"Wait and see, I guess. I'd better get busy. I promised Kellen I'd have sketches by—"

"Kellen? He was there? I thought one of his gofers was meeting you."

"A Mr. Winslow was at the house when I arrived, but Kellen came in later because whatever they were doing for the movie got rained out."

"And you call him Kellen?" Paul frowned.

"That's his name."

"I know that! I mean, isn't it rather . . . familiar?"

"Oh, Paul." Paige laughed. "You sound like a disapproving father. I frequently have a first-name relationship with my clients."

"Well, just remember who and what Kellen Davis is."

"Meaning?"

"He's a womanizer, Paige. He'd gobble up a lovely, decent girl like you for breakfast. He didn't try to hustle you, did he? Hey, we don't need this job."

"Paul, for heaven's sake," Paige said. "Kellen Davis was a perfect gentleman." True, she thought. He was perfect. He was gentle. And he was most definitely a man. Oh, Paige, shut up.

"Why are you smiling?"

"Because you are silly and I adore you," she said, getting up and heading for the door. "Ta-ta, sweet Paul. I must go earn my keep."

As she was about to enter her office Paige remembered she had not asked Janet if there had been any messages and walked instead to the secretary's desk. The young girl was not there, but Paige retrieved several pink slips of paper. Her glance fell on the movie magazine spread open to the story on Kellen Davis and, after looking around quickly to see that no one was observing her, Paige picked it up.

There was a full-page color photograph of Kellen standing on the deck of a sailboat. He wore only rough-edged cutoff jeans, and his hair appeared tousled by the wind as he squinted slightly against the glare off the water. His bare, massive chest was covered in curly black hair and a medallion hung from a long gold chain around his neck. Wide shoulders tapered to a narrow waist, and the muscles in his thighs looked tight and corded.

Paige's eyes were drawn to the soft lips that were flashing a smile over the straight white teeth. Unconsciously she placed her fingertips on her own lips as she recalled the moment when Kellen had claimed her mouth in that searing embrace that had sent her senses swirling out of control.

Forcing herself to come back to the present, Paige scanned the article on the opposite page. It had indeed been rumored that an affair had taken place between twenty-two-year-old Hildy Holt and Kellen Davis, thirty-six, during the filming of *Master's Touch*. Although the journalist stated that neither star would admit to the liaison, it was definitely true that Miss Holt was presently in seclusion in Paris, apparently sulking over having been rejected by Kellen for the captivating redhead, Felicia Evans. Miss Evans was to star in Kellen's newest picture, to be filmed on location in the Phoenix area, and it was common knowledge that Felicia was presently the recipient of Mr. Davis's affections.

"No wonder he's so eager to get a bed," Paige muttered, tossing the magazine back onto the desk. "Felicia Evans probably isn't the type to camp out on the floor. Lord, the man changes women faster than shirts!"

Paige stomped back to her office and sank into her desk chair. What was she getting upset about? she thought suddenly. She certainly didn't give diddly about how many women Kellen Davis lured into his bed. Lured? Ha! He probably had to beat them off with a stick! The more she thought about it, the more she convinced herself that he was arrogant and rude. How dare he just march up, take her in his arms, and kiss her! He might get away with that kind of aggressive behavior in the movies, but this was real life! In another era he'd have been labeled a cad. Today he was a rat fink! But she was wise to him now. He wouldn't get away with that again!

With a determined nod Paige pulled her notes from her briefcase and began the tedious procedure of developing a thorough picture of her ideas for the decorating of Kellen Davis's living room. It was more difficult than usual as she had no idea what she might find in the way of furniture already in stock in the exclusive shops she would visit. Supplies would be depleted because of the Christmas buying season, and she could only hope she would be able to purchase items that would please the movie star. Several hours later she was almost halfway completed with her task when Paul sauntered into her office.

"Quitting time," he said. "How's the project going?"

"Slow. It's difficult because I don't really know what's left out there."

"Well, Davis will have to understand that you're not a miracle worker. His big rush order is pretty unreasonable, if you ask me."

"I'll do the best I can. I'll finish these sketches tonight."

"How about dinner? In the mood for Chinese food?"

"No, thank you, Paul. I have several more hours of work to do yet. I'd better go straight home and get at it."

"You don't have to put in overtime for Davis," Paul said, scowling slightly. "He can wait for his grand decor just like everyone else."

"I don't mind," she said, placing her supplies in her briefcase. "Oh, I won't be here in the morning. I'll set out right from home to find Mr. Sex Symbol of America a bed. I'll check in with you sometime during the day."

"What happened to his old bed? Did he wear it out?"

"Now, Paul, that wasn't nice. The man can't help it if women find him irresistible. It's just a cross he has to bear," she teased.

"I should have such burdens," Paul said, rolling his eyes to the heavens.

"You do all right with the fair sex. Good night. Quit frowning. Talk to you tomorrow."

"Just remember that Davis has no principles when it comes to women, Paige. He's a user who—"

"Good night!" She waved as she left the office.

The air was damp and chilly as Paige eased her car into the heavy traffic on Central Avenue. Forty-five minutes later she pulled into her slot in the parking lot of the high-rise apartment building she lived in. It was on the edge of the bustling college town of Tempe and her close proximity to the Arizona State University campus afforded her easy access to the theater productions, lectures, and many other ongoing activities. She attended these regularly with carefully selected men from the many who sought her company.

As she was unlocking her apartment door she heard her telephone ringing. She rushed to answer it, tossing her belongings onto the sofa.

"Hello?" she said breathlessly.

"Paige?"

"Yes."

"This is Kellen. Did I get you out of the shower?"

"No, I just rushed through the door straight from the office," she said, her mind racing with wonder at why Kellen Davis was calling her.

"Your Paul is a slave driver," he said, his voice rich and deep.

"He's not mine and he's a very nice boss," she said, knowing she sounded defensive. "Was there something I could do for you?"

"Don't hand me a loaded question like *that*." He chuckled, the throaty resonance causing Paige to smile. "I actually called to ask a favor of you."

"Oh?"

"When you buy my bed tomorrow, do you suppose—just suppose—you could get me some sheets and pillows and blankets? Oh, and a bedspread? Please, Paige, please?"

"You sound like a little boy who wants an extra cookie," she said.

"But, Paige, what good will a bed do me if I don't have the stuff to make it up? Take pity on me."

And Felicia? she thought. Whew! That was bitchy. "All right, Kellen. Any particular kind of sheets?"

"Not satin, for heaven's sake. They stick to me. Just plain old ordinary material and some nice mushy pillows."

"Mushy?"

"Yeah, soft and . . . mushy."

"I'll see what I can find," she said, a wide smile on her face. "Do your fans know you sleep on mushy pillows?"

"I don't think so. I wonder if that would blow my image? Listen, I really appreciate this. Thank you."

"You're welcome."

"And Paige? I'm looking forward to seeing you tomorrow. Good night."

"Good night, Kellen."

Paige slowly replaced the receiver and stared at it for several moments. A world-famous movie star was sitting around worrying about not having any sheets and blankets? And he wanted mushy pillows? It was enough to make a person think the man was a regular human being. However, he was not, Paige warned herself. He was Kellen Davis and that spelled danger in big bold letters.

Paige turned on the end-table lamp, which sent a warm glow over the dark room. The main area was a good size for one person, and for her color scheme she had chosen soft shades of mint green and pale yellow. After living in Colorado, Paige found the heat of Phoenix oppressive when she'd first arrived, and she had been determined to bring a sense of coolness to the apartment. She had brought none of the furnishings from the house she had shared with Jerry Cunningham, having wanted a totally fresh start in her new location as she began rebuilding her shattered life.

Her bedroom matched the decor of the living room except for a rich kelly-green spread on the double bed. The material had reminded her of a plush, inviting field of grass, and she loved its rich texture. She changed into a fluffy robe, then made a quick supper of soup and a salad, which she consumed in a rush. She put the dishes she'd used in the dishwasher and flicked it into action. Curled up in the corner on the sofa, she resumed her work on the sketches for Kellen.

At midnight she stretched lazily and yawned. She had completed two totally different sets of pictures for Kellen Davis's review. One used conventional-size sofas and the other used love seats on the chance she might not find furniture to his liking. Placing the papers carefully in her briefcase, Paige turned off the light and walked to the bedroom, suddenly aware of her fatigue.

Snuggling under the blankets, she sighed wearily and rearranged her pillow, wondering with a soft laugh, just before she fell asleep, if Kellen would consider her own pillow mushy enough. Several hours later she sat bolt up in the bed, wide-awake and trembling. A haunting dream had plagued her and she turned on the lamp to bring comforting light into the room.

She had seen Jerry's face. He had been laughing, though there was no sound, and she had pleaded with him to listen to her. He had brushed her away and disappeared into a foggy haze that she had stumbled through searching for him, screaming his name. But then a tall figure had emerged and taken her gently by the hand, leading her to a bright patch of sunlight.

"It was Kellen," she whispered. "He found me and brought me back."

Shaken by the strange scenario that had invaded her subconscious, Paige pulled on her robe over her filmy nightgown and went into the kitchen. She fixed a mug of hot chocolate and sipped it as she leaned against the counter. Hoping the soothing drink would quiet her jangled nerves, she returned to bed, only to toss and turn through the hours that remained of the long, lonely night.

Her head ached from lack of sleep and neither her morning shower nor several cups of coffee revived her. She pulled on boots with a brown corduroy slacks-and-blazer set, to which she had added a burnt-orange turtleneck sweater. Deciding her head could not withstand the tight hairstyle of her chignon, she brushed her heavy dark tresses into a wavy cascade that fell just below her shoulders. She preferred the more severe appearance the bun presented, feeling it made her seem more sophisticated and older, but this morning she did not particularly care.

In an automatic gesture Paige checked her wallet to see that she had the charge card from the House of Martin. She would use it to purchase whatever struck her fancy as she shopped for Kellen Davis. A reputation for paying bills promptly had afforded Paul's firm an enormous credit line at the most prestigious stores in Phoenix and in the surrounding suburbs.

A bleak Arizona sun seemed determined to stake its claim to the day. The rain clouds were beating a hasty retreat over the mountains against the horizon as Paige drove out of Tempe and along Scottsdale Road to the quaint little town of the same name. Two hours and three stores later she slid into a booth in a small café and ordered a cup of coffee. Nothing, she thought gloomily. Either the bedroom suites were too feminine or they couldn't deliver for at least a week or they had a bed but no dressers or vice versa. Her feet hurt. Her head ached. Kellen Davis was a spoiled brat, demanding his bed be there today. And if she *did* find it, she still had to go buy his damnable mushy pillows!

Her next stop was a large store on the edge of town with carpeting so thick, it was difficult for Paige to maneuver in her high-heeled boots. She was greeted warmly by William Tate, the owner, who stroked his chin thoughtfully at her request.

"Well," he said, "I have a hand-carved king-size bed with an upright chest of drawers and a dresser with a mirror. There's also two end tables. It was a custom order and the dear woman's husband died before it was finished. It's fantastically expensive because it took the craftsman over six months to complete."

"Show me," Paige said firmly, and moments later added, "I'll take it if you can deliver today."

"I like doing business with you, Paige," William said with a laugh. "You get right to the point. I'll have it out of here this afternoon. This is really a gorgeous set but still, it looks masculine. Who's your client?"

"Kellen Davis."

"The movie star?"

"That's the one."

"I'll be damned. You *are* moving in fancy circles these days, love. I read in the newspapers that he was in town making a picture. I take it you've met him?"

"Yes."

"And?"

"He's very nice." She shrugged.

"I'll bet." William chuckled. "Let's go do the paperwork on this stuff since you obviously aren't going to share any sordid tidbits about the decadent Mr. Davis."

"For heaven's sake, William." Paige scowled as she followed the laughing man across the room.

After arranging the delivery of the furniture for two o'clock, Paige hurried to her car and drove to Goldwater's, where she made a beeline for the bedding department. She selected two sets of sheets and pillowcases, one tan, the other with tiny tan-and-blue checks. The blankets were royal blue and brown, and the bedspread a rich velour in large diamond shapes of off-white, tan, blue, and chocolate. The carpeting in Kellen's bedroom had been a light beige, and Paige was sure the colors would work well together. Everything was running smoothly until she stood in front of the stack of pillows. With a resigned sigh she began to squeeze each one under the watchful eye of the saleswoman.

"These," Paige said finally. "They're really mushy. I mean, soft."

"Cash or charge?" the woman asked, obviously relieved that Paige was finished mauling the merchandise.

Paige ate a hamburger, French fries, and a milk shake and two aspirins for dessert at a fast food restaurant, keeping her car in view out the window. The small trunk had not held all the bedding, and the remainder was piled on the backseat. Sliding behind the wheel, she gingerly massaged her aching temples and was definitely not smiling as she drove out of town and headed for the home of Mr. Kellen Davis. A car she assumed to be Timmy Winslow's was parked in front of the impressive structure, and she knocked on the heavy door rather than using the key Kellen had given her.

"Mrs. Cunningham," Timmy said when he answered her summons, "do come in."

"I have to unload my car," she said. "Just pretend I'm not here yet."

"Don't be silly, I'll give you a hand. What goodies do you have?"

"Bedding."

"I do hope you found soft pillows for Kellen. He's very particular about that."

"Believe me, they are mushy!"

"I see he already spoke with you about it. He's the only one I know who uses that word." Timmy chortled merrily.

Within a few minutes the purchases were in the corner of the living room and Paige accepted Timmy's offer of a cup of coffee after insisting he call her by her first name.

"With pleasure," he said, "and you shall refer to me as Timmy, as does the world."

Paige was unable to resist the infectious personality of the older gentleman and found herself relaxing in his company. "Have you worked for Kellen long?" she asked as they sat at the rickety table in the kitchen.

"A dozen years. I was there when he made his first picture and every one since then. I was also in attendance when he won the Oscar last year. That was quite a night. I do a little bit of everything for Kellen, but foremost I consider myself his friend."

"I think that's lovely," Paige said, smiling warmly. "He's very fortunate to have you."

"No, I'm the lucky one. Kellen is a complicated man, Paige. He's not what he's presented as being. The image the public worships is far from the Kellen Davis I know."

"I don't understand."

"Paige, dear, I must run. I hate to be rude but I have a million errands. Will you be all right here alone?"

"Of course. The delivery men will be arriving soon and I'll lock up when I leave."

"Splendid. We'll continue our discussion another time. Take care."

"Good-bye, Timmy."

What had Timmy meant? Paige thought as she sat in the quiet room. Kellen was not what he seemed to be? No one could deny he was handsome. He wasn't a Romeo? Of course, he was. Everyone knew that! Now she was curious and hoped to get a chance to talk to Timmy again soon.

The delivery men arrived on time and were impressed with the fact that they were bringing a bed for the great Kellen Davis. They whispered and snickered among themselves, and Paige was quite convinced the topic of conversation was the use the star would make of this particular piece of furniture.

It took three trips up the long staircase for Paige to get all the supplies she had purchased to the bedroom, and she was angry at herself for not asking the burly men to accomplish the task before they had left the house. Their truck had long since disappeared down the driveway when she pulled the checked sheets out of the wrapper and tugged and tucked them into place. The pillowcases were next, and then she smoothed the blankets over the large expanse. She smiled in approval at the effect the spread had on the room and sat down wearily on the edge of the bed, deciding it was a job well done.

"I wonder what mushy pillows feel like," she said, glancing in their direction. On impulse she stretched out on the bed and lowered her head slowly onto the marshmallow-soft mound. "Heavenly," she murmured. "Maybe if I close my eyes for ten minutes this headache will go away. Lord, I'm so tired," she said, and fell instantly asleep.

Two hours later Kellen pulled into the driveway, a

smile crossing his handsome face when he saw the car in front of the house. Paige was there, he thought. Hopefully that meant he had a bed. He wondered if she'd seem so . . . special today. Maybe she'd just made a strange first impression on him, and he'd realize she was simply a lovely woman but certainly no more than that. Still, there was something about her that he couldn't figure out. "Paige?" he called, coming in the front door.

After poking his head into the empty kitchen, Kellen retraced his steps through the living room and bounded up the stairs two at a time. He strode down the corridor to his bedroom, then stopped perfectly still when he viewed the scene before him. Moving cautiously forward, he stood by the edge of the bed, shoving his hands deep into his pockets as he gazed at the sleeping woman.

She looked like a child, he thought. A sweet, innocent, vulnerable little girl. He'd known her hair would be beautiful down around her face. He'd just known it. She looked good there, in his bed, peaceful and sleeping. Lord, she'd be great to wake up to in the morning. He'd like to— Slow down, he told himself. Just wake her up. But how? He'd kiss those luscious lips and— No! He could wiggle her toe or something. Maybe he'd—

As if sensing a presence in the room, Paige opened her eyes and stared at Kellen for a moment as if not really seeing him. Then as the fogginess of sleep dissipated, she gasped and sat bolt up on the bed.

"Oh, no," she whispered.

"Now, don't get excited," Kellen said, holding up his hands and backing up several steps.

"What am I . . . ? Why are you . . . ? Oh, no." She glanced quickly at her watch. "I can't believe I did this!"

"What did you do?" he asked.

"I slept in your bed!" she yelled, getting up and tugging her sweater into place.

"Not in it really." He grinned. "Just kind of on it. That was a good test. Looks like you bought me a beauty."

"I'm so embarrassed. I've never done anything so unprofessional before in my whole career."

He chuckled. "I won't tell anyone. I promise."

"This really isn't funny. I apologize for my . . . breach in etiquette," she said primly.

"Oh. I see. Well, I accept," he said, trying unsuccessfully to suppress the smile that was creeping onto the corners of his mouth. "This is a fantastic bedroom, Paige. I really like it. Thanks for doing a super job."

"I can vouch for the pillows," she said miserably.

"Hey, cheer up. So you took a nap. Big deal. That means you'll be all full of vim and vigor for our dinner date."

"Oh, no! I didn't call Paul! May I use your phone?"

"Sure. There's only the one downstairs right now."

"Thank you. I really am sorry about playing Goldilocks, Kellen," she said, hurrying from the room.

Paul, Kellen thought. He didn't know him, but Paul sure as hell was getting on his nerves!

Kellen walked slowly down the stairs just as Paige was hanging up the telephone that sat on the floor in the corner of the living room. She turned and watched as he approached, his massive frame seeming to overwhelm her as he came to where she stood.

"I had better be going," she said, looking up at him.

"I'll pick you up at seven. I thought we'd go to the Majestic."

"Oh," she said, her eyes widening slightly at the name of the expensive restaurant. "We'll review the plans for this room when you come to my apartment."

"Fine. Paige, would you wear your hair down like that tonight?"

"I . . . well, yes, I guess so."

"Good." He smiled. "I'll see you later."

"All right, Kellen." She hurried to the entryway and out the front door.

Like a fawn, Kellen thought as he watched her leave. A frightened, beautiful brown-eyed young deer. My, he was getting poetic in his old age, Kellen told himself. One thing was certain: Paige Cunningham was every bit as special today as she had been yesterday. He'd just see her tonight and then call it quits. Kellen had a feeling he might be getting in over his head, and he didn't need that kind of trouble.

At her apartment Paige shed her clothing and pinned her thick hair on top of her head before sinking up to her chin in a hot bubble bath. She frowned as she thought of the embarrassing episode at Kellen's. She had actually snoozed away in blissful slumber on the movie star's bed.

She amazed herself sometimes, she thought. How could she do such a stupid thing? Kellen had certainly taken it in stride. She supposed having women stretched out on his bed was no new event for him. If Paul had known, he'd croak! She hated lying to Paul, but what choice did she have? He seemed to accept the explanation that the delivery had been delayed. But what about herself? First she'd responded to Kellen's kiss like a wanton woman. Then she'd slept in—no, *on*—his bed. What would she do for Act Three? Nothing, that's what. She'd go out for dinner with him tonight and it would be strictly business—just as every encounter would be from now on.

She blow-dried her freshly shampooed hair, and the dark tresses glowed in the light from her dressing table as she applied a pale lip gloss and a dab of perfume at the base of her throat. Her dress was a street-length yellow chiffon with long sheer sleeves that fastened at the wrist with tiny pearl buttons. The matching belt nipped in her tiny waist and she added a gold locket to the rounded neckline. She slipped on thin-strapped evening sandals, then stared at her reflection in the mirror. Her large dark eyes seemed to sparkle strangely, to be curiously alive as she leaned closer for a better look.

She was just very wide-awake, she finally told herself. After all, she'd had an afternoon nap!

The knock at the door came a few minutes before seven, and she answered it with slightly trembling hands. She was nervous all of a sudden and had no idea why. The evening with Kellen was centered on business, with dinner only an afterthought due to the necessity of them both needing a meal. Whom was she kidding? she thought. One didn't go to the Majestic on a whim. Come to think of it though, Kellen Davis probably did. Relax, Paige told herself. This was no momentous occasion for him.

"Hello, Kellen," she said, stepping back to allow him to enter. Oh, no, she thought, he got better and better. There should be a law against shoulders that wide, hair so thick, eyes a fathomless blue, features so handsome and rugged.

"You look lovely, Paige," Kellen said as she closed the door.

"So do you." She smiled, glancing at his perfectly cut dark suit, dark tie, and blue shirt that matched his eyes perfectly.

"Thank you, I think." He chuckled. "I don't believe I've ever been called lovely before."

"Would you care for a drink while we go over the drawings?"

"If you're having one."

"White wine, Scotch, vodka . . . ?"

"Scotch is fine. On the rocks."

"Make yourself at home. I'll be right back."

Kellen settled himself on the sofa and glanced around the pretty room, nodding in approval at what he saw. He thanked Paige for the drink she handed him and watched as she moved gracefully across the carpet to retrieve her papers from the desk against the far wall. As she sat down next to him the filmy layers of the skirt of her dress lifted in the air and draped themselves over Kellen's leg.

"Sorry," she said, laughing slightly. "I look like a yellow parachute."

As she slid her hand under the material to brush it down between them, her fingertips trailed along Kellen's solid thigh. He took a quick intake of breath as the feathery touch set off a sudden rush of heated desire through his lower body. His eyes flew to Paige's face, and he was immediately aware she had no idea of the sensations she had caused to surge through him, nor had the action been a provocative move on her part. He cleared his throat and took a large swallow of his Scotch. An inner anger gripped him at the effect Paige's fleeting touch had had on him. He felt foolish and actually embarrassed that he was so physically vulnerable to her. Even more, it was confusing, and he scowled at his drink.

"Kellen?" Paige said. "Is something wrong?"

"Pardon? Oh, no, of course not."

"Well," she said, handing him the papers, "here are my ideas. I must tell you, Kellen, that if what I found when I was shopping for your bedroom suite is any indication of the low stock because of Christmas, we may have a real problem on our hands."

"I see."

"I'm trying to have an alternate plan in case I simply can't find things, but you'd have to agree to it. I wish you could go with me because I may have to resort to some unusual pieces, and I'd really like to know if you approve. Of course, that's impossible so—"

"No, it's not."

"But aren't you busy with the movie?"

"We really haven't started the picture yet. I've been here a week with the director and a skeleton crew of technicians, going over details and checking what will be needed for outside shots. The rest of the actors, cameramen, the whole crowd will be arriving in a few days."

"But you're the star. Why do you have to be involved in the preliminary work?"

"I own this picture. I started my company when we did *Master's Touch*. This film is the second endeavor by Davis Productions. The point is, everything is under control. I'd enjoy shopping with you if I wouldn't be in the way."

"That's marvelous," she said, smiling. "I've been so worried that if I had to go to extremes you'd absolutely hate it. This way you'll be right there to help decide. I'll steer you in the right direction as far as colors and— Can you go tomorrow?"

"Sure. Your eyes are just dancing," he said, grinning.

"This is exciting! We'll create a beautiful living room for you, Kellen."

"Sounds great." Lord, he thought, she was all charged up over furniture. The fact that they'd be together all day certainly hadn't had any thrilling impact on her. What had happened to not seeing her after tonight? He'd opened his big mouth, that's what. "Since we've completed our business," he said, "shall we go to dinner?"

"I'll get my coat," she said, getting up and walking across the room and into the bedroom. Oh, dear, she thought, she'd gotten carried away. She had been so concerned there would be difficulties over her selections that she'd completely forgotten her resolve to avoid being close to Kellen. It would be all right. She'd drag him through every furniture store in town and he'd be bored to tears. Selecting sofas and chairs was not exactly a romantic interlude. "All set," she said as she reentered the living room.

"My chariot awaits," he said, getting to his feet. "Actually it's a rented car, but it will get us where we're going."

The car was large, the interior plush, and Kellen commanded the powerful vehicle with ease and confidence.

"The Christmas decorations certainly make everything festive," he said. "I love this holiday, don't you?"

"Not particularly," Paige said. "I think it's meant for families. People who are alone have nothing to celebrate."

Kellen frowned. "You had a very bitter edge to your voice when you said that, Paige. Didn't you ever believe in Santa Claus?"

"A long time ago, Kellen," she said softly, staring at her hands, which were clutched tightly in her lap. "But not anymore. I'm all grown up now."

"That doesn't matter. Santa Claus is more of an attitude really. There's presents to give and cookies to bake, parties to attend and carols to sing. Don't you enjoy any part of it, Paige?"

"No. Could we change the subject, please?"

"Sure." He shrugged. So Mrs. Cunningham was a Scrooge, he thought. Something told him she'd felt that way only since she'd become a widow. Didn't like Christmas, huh? Well, he'd just see about that!

A smug smile crossed Kellen Davis's face, and he suddenly felt happier than he had in a long time, although he had absolutely no idea why.

Three

The wave of depression that had swept over Paige during their talk about Christmas dissipated into thin air the moment the Majestic came into view.

"I feel like Cinderella," she said, laughing suddenly. "I've never been here before, so if I gawk, just tell me to close my mouth."

"One reason I eat at the Majestic is because I know the owner," Kellen said. "He makes sure I'm not pestered for autographs all evening. As for you, be just as wide-eyed as you like. It will be fun showing it to you for the first time. I hope you're hungry. The food is superb."

"I'm starving."

The moment they stepped inside the grand building, they were descended upon by a beaming man who ushered them quickly out of the main area and into an enormous room that was cozily lit by candles set in the middle of the tables. They were led to a window table against the far wall, where they could see the lights of Phoenix sparkling like thousands of fireflies. The man snapped his fingers and ordered the wine steward to report front and center. Kellen rattled off the name of a French wine, and the uniformed waiter bowed and disappeared.

Paige knew she was smiling as she took in the elegance of her surroundings. She had dated several men who had been willing to go to any cost to show her a good time, but never had she been anyplace that compared to the Majestic. Nothing had been spared. The china was wafer-thin, the utensils sterling silver, the glasses finely cut crystal. The service was impeccable, and to top it off she was sitting across the table from Kellen Davis, the heartthrob of America, who was handsome, charming, and witty.

In what appeared to be a prearranged agreement Kellen signed his name to a half dozen menus at the beginning of the meal and they were not again disturbed by autograph-seeking fans. They chatted comfortably throughout dinner, and over coffee Kellen asked Paige how she had chosen her life's work.

"You've done very well for someone so young," he said. "The House of Martin is certainly well-known."

"I'm not *that* young," she said.

"Twenty-five, twenty-six?"

"Seven."

He smiled. "With your hair loose around your face you appear very youthful."

"Which is why I wear it in a bun most of the time. It's difficult to convince some of the matriarchs of this town I know what I'm doing when I look like a kid."

"What do old ladies with blue hair know?"

"Fact remains, they're the ones with the houses to decorate and the money to do it."

"What about me? Don't I count?"

"You certainly do." She smiled. "You're a very important client. Paul was very pleased you selected our firm."

Paul again, he thought. They weren't going to start talking about that guy again. "Do you think we'll have time to shop for books tomorrow?" he asked.

"I don't know. It depends on how difficult our hunt for furniture becomes. You can always give me a list of what authors you prefer."

"But I love to browse in bookstores," he said.

"You do?" she asked in surprise, recalling the many Saturday afternoons she had spent pleasurable hours doing just that. "So do I."

"Maybe we should set aside a block of time. It could end up being a lot of fun," he said. "But for now, let's go into the other room and dance. The band is supposed to be excellent."

"I . . . all right."

Kellen signaled for the waiter, who materialized instantly with the check on a gold engraved plate. Kellen paid by credit card, then pushed back his chair. Paige rose to join him, and with his fingertips resting lightly on her elbow, he escorted her to a large room where dimly lit chandeliers hung from the ceiling. A twelve-piece band was playing lilting music as they walked to a small table. Kellen ordered drinks from a passing waitress and then extended his hand to Paige.

In thirty seconds she was going to be in his arms, Paige thought wildly as they walked onto the floor. She must be crazy. He was dangerous to her equilibrium. He threw her off-balance, unsettled her. She knew it was simply a physical thing, but it was scary. That was a childish word, but it was the only one she could come up with! If she had any intelligence at all, she'd plead a headache and ask him to take her home. So much for her brain.

Kellen drew her close, his large hand resting on her waist as he moved her smoothly across the floor in perfect rhythm to the music. She could feel his warm breath on her forehead and the heat from his touch through the thin material of her dress. She was aware of his musky after-shave and a lingering soapy fragrance emanating from his body. He was remarkably agile for a man his size, Paige noticed, and she seemed to fit perfectly against the hard contours of his frame. But still she stiffened slightly when he pulled her closer.

"I'm not going to bite you, Little Red Riding Hood," he said quietly.

"So said the Big Bad Wolf," she muttered into his shirt.

"Is that what you think I am?"

"Well . . ."

"The shoe would have to fit before I could wear it, Paige. It doesn't."

"Read any good movie magazines lately?" she said, knowing she sounded bitchy, but not seeming to be able to keep the cutting edge from her voice.

"That does it," he growled. He dropped his hand from her waist and led her from the dance floor. Paige had to hurry to keep up, and her eyes were wide with surprise. "Now," he said when they were once again seated at the table, "just what was that remark supposed to mean? You don't actually believe the garbage they write in those things, do you?"

"I'm not in the habit of reading them," she snapped. "My secretary happened to show me an article concerning you and Hildy Holt and—"

"Don't tell me, let me guess. Hildy and I had an affair while filming *Master's Touch*."

"You did?" Paige said, a frown crossing her face.

"Nope."

"But everyone thinks that you did."

"Because that's what they want to believe. Oh, Paige, don't you see? It goes with the turf. I'm presented to the public as Mr. Macho. It was an image created by my agent years ago when I made my first picture. Kellen Davis is a ladies' man, a playboy. I love 'em, I leave 'em. Women are supposed to fantasize about being the one who will finally bring me to my knees. It's all worked well for me at the box office, but it doesn't mean that's who I really am. Hey, I'm no monk, but if I slept with as many women as they claim, I'd be too exhausted to work."

Paige leaned back in her chair and crossed her arms over her breasts. She studied Kellen's face, squinting slightly as if deep in thought. "What about Hildy Holt sulking in Paris since you've taken up with Felicia Evans?" she asked finally.

"Your Honor"—he chuckled softly—"Hildy Holt went to France to be with her pregnant sister, who is having some medical problems. As for Felicia, we're dear, close friends, and I'm delighted we'll be filming another picture together. The problem is doing love scenes with her. She usually dissolves in a fit of laughter because she says it's like being in bed with her brother. Any other questions?"

"Oh, Kellen." Paige sighed. "How do I know if you're telling the truth? But I suppose it's really none of my business anyway."

"Yes, it is," he said, leaning forward and taking her hand between his two large ones. "Paige, I rarely care what people think of me. I know who I am, and my true friends are aware that a false picture has been presented to the public and they know why it's necessary. I'm not sure why, but it's very important to me that you do believe me, or at least give me a chance to prove to you that I'm not what I'm set up to be."

"Why?"

"Lord, you're making this tough." He raked his

hand through his hair in a frustrated gesture. "Hell, I don't know. I would like us to get better acquainted, but we can't if you automatically peg me as an egotistical slob who uses women with no regard for their feelings. You're a beautiful, desirable woman, Paige, but I'll never take anything from you that you're not willing to give."

Paige blinked her eyes once slowly as she stared at Kellen. Her mind did a tug-of-war, part of her declaring his words sincere, the other screaming at her that this man was a professional actor capable of producing any emotional scene to perfection. "For now," she said firmly, "the jury is still out. Would you care to dance, Mr. Davis?"

Thank God, he thought, grinning as he rose to join her. He was still in the ballgame. He didn't know why he even wanted to play in this one, but there was just something about her that was getting under his skin. Maybe he'd feel better in the morning and come to his senses.

For reasons she couldn't explain Paige relaxed in Kellen's arms the moment he swept her into his embrace. Within minutes he had cradled her hand in his and brought it to his chest, where she could feel the steady beat of his heart.

Tonight she *was* Cinderella, she decided, and nothing would spoil it. She had no more mental energies to sort out the confusing picture surrounding Kellen Davis. He was rapidly becoming an enigma, a complicated mystery that she would deal with later. But not now. Not yet. The music was slow and seductive, and she was in the arms of an incredibly handsome man. She felt feminine, pretty, and alive, and she relished the sensations. She wouldn't dwell on anything tonight except her beautiful surroundings and the man she was with.

Again Kellen's masculine aroma reached her, and

she was totally aware of the hardness of his chest, thighs, and shoulders. The song ended, another began, and they danced on. Time had no place in this scenario, Paige mused. Reality was slipping away, as were the other people in the room, the noise of clinking glasses, and the murmur of voices. She was floating on a cloud with Kellen in a world occupied only by them. She was being foolish and impractical—totally unlike herself—and she didn't care. A soft sigh of contentment escaped from her lips and Kellen moved back slightly to look down at her questioningly.

"Tired?" he asked softly.

"Oh, no," she whispered. "I'm having a lovely time. Don't forget, I had an afternoon nap."

"True." He chuckled softly. "We dance well together, Paige. They should put us in the movies."

"Heaven forbid." She smiled up at him. "Haven't you heard? That Hollywood crowd is a horrible bunch. The movie magazines are full of their escapades."

"Scandalous." He nodded. "You're right, we'll have nothing to do with them. We'll remain who we really are. You're Paige Cunningham, talented decorator, and I'm—"

"Who are you, Kellen?" she asked quietly.

"Kellen Davis, who works for a living and leaves his job behind when he comes home at night. I'm a man, a human being who wants a little happiness and peace in his life like anyone else. An ordinary person really, with hopes and dreams, laughter and tears."

Smiling, Paige nestled closer to him and felt his arms tighten around her slender frame. He kissed her gently on the forehead, and his lips remained there, soft and warm against her skin. They hardly moved, only swaying slightly to the enchanting music, and the time slipped away.

With a drumroll the band concluded the final number, and the chandeliers came up to full power. Paige blinked in surprise as if coming out of a trance and automatically disengaged herself from Kellen's embrace. "I think they're trying to tell us something," she said, smiling slightly.

"All good things," he said, circling her shoulders with his arm and leading her from the room.

He retrieved her coat from the checkroom and stopped once again to shake the hand of the beaming owner of the Majestic. A few words to the parking attendant brought their plush car roaring to the front steps of the restaurant. When they were seated inside it, Kellen extended his hand to Paige. She moved across the seat and rested her head on his shoulder. They rode in silence, each lost in his and her own thoughts, and did not speak until Paige handed him her key at her apartment door.

"I'll see you in," he said quietly.

Paige flicked on the light switch inside the door, spreading a glow over the pretty room from the lamps on the end tables. She dropped her coat onto a chair and turned to face Kellen, who had advanced only a few feet into the apartment.

What now? Paige thought nervously. She had to say something. "Kellen, I had such a marvelous time," she managed, her voice disconcertingly husky. "Thank you so much."

"I enjoyed the evening too," he said, his voice even huskier. "What time should I pick you up in the morning to go shopping?"

Shopping? Oh, right, Kellen's living room. "You're the client, remember? I'll drive."

"I've seen your car, Paige. I don't fit in those very well. I'll have my knees in my mouth."

She laughed. "You've got a point there. All right. Nine o'clock?"

"Fine."

Their eyes met and held. In seemingly slow motion each moved toward the other in an undeniable urge to claim what was theirs. Paige lifted her arms to circle Kellen's neck as he pulled her against him. His hands flattened against her back as he lowered his head and claimed her mouth in a searing kiss that seemed endless. His lips parted hers, his tongue seeking and finding the warmth of hers. Paige moaned as she molded herself to the hard contours of Kellen's body. His hands inched upward, sliding to her full breasts, which responded immediately to his gentle caresses.

The only sound in the room was their labored, raspy breathing as their mouths continued to ravish each other's in feverishly hungry kisses. Paige could feel the evidence of Kellen's desire pressing against her as she sank her fingertips deeper into his thick raven hair, urging him closer. Her knees were trembling as a wave of passion swept through her. Her body was crying out to be fulfilled, to be given what it had been denied for so long. She wanted Kellen. She needed what his masculinity could provide, but it was more than that. It could not be just any man; it must be Kellen. Kellen would quell the burning flame of passion that consumed her. Only Kellen. Only him.

"My God," he whispered huskily, disengaging her arms from his neck. "I want you so much, Paige. But I asked you to trust me, believe in me. I can't run the risk of frightening you away."

"Kellen, I—"

"Good night, pretty Paige," he said softly, kissing her gently on the forehead. "I'll see you in a few hours."

She could only nod and watch him close the door quietly behind him. Her fingertips came to rest on her throbbing lips. The room seemed suddenly large, cold, and empty without Kellen, and with a sigh she turned off the lights and walked slowly into the bedroom. Minutes later she was clad in her nightie, lying beneath the blankets and staring up at a ceiling she could not see in the darkness.

She wasn't sorry, she thought adamantly. She wanted, needed, to be kissed and held by Kellen. He made her feel alive again, whole. Nothing would come of it—jet-setting movie stars and southwestern interior decorators didn't mix well. They were worlds apart. But until the rest of the movie people arrived, Kellen was separated from his normal world. She'd enjoy the hours they'd share, cherish them. That was all she'd ask of him—a little time together to allow her femininity to resurface, to hear the melodic sound of her own laughter. She'd fill her inner soul with Kellen and have those memories as a buffer against Christmas when it came. In a way she'd be using him, but she was sure he wasn't seriously interested in her. He was just bored, waiting for the shooting of the movie to start, Paige reasoned. They'd have two or three days. A brief interlude . . . a lifetime for her . . . and that would be enough.

The next morning Paige dressed in gray flannel slacks and a fluffy pink sweater. She brushed her hair into a glossy cascade and pushed her feet into soft leather loafers. Her experience told her that she and Kellen might tromp around for hours in search of appropriate furniture for his living room and the last thing she needed was aching feet. She felt exhilarated and full of energy, despite the short night's sleep, and humming softly, she set coffee on to perk.

Paige smiled brightly when a knock sounded at the door, and she greeted Kellen cheerfully when he stepped into the room.

"Good morning to you too," he said, looking

devastatingly handsome in black cords and a red V-neck sweater over an open-collar white shirt.

"I was just going to have a cup of coffee. Will you join me?"

"Sounds good."

Kellen followed her into the small kitchen and sat at the dinette table that was only big enough for two. Paige was aware of his eyes following her as she reached up to pull mugs out of the cupboard. She could smell the familiar after-shave and was acutely aware of his presence, which seemed to fill the tiny room. When she turned, she knew his gaze would meet hers and she was glad. Glad he was there with her for the numbered hours they would share. He *was* looking at her as she brought the steaming mugs to the table and sat opposite him. She smiled warmly as she allowed herself yet another quick glance at his wide shoulders and broad chest outlined in the obviously expensive sweater.

"So how was your bed?" she asked, stirring a teaspoon of sugar into her coffee.

"I died and went to heaven. It was excellent."

"Pillows mushy enough?"

"Right on the money."

"Good. Let's hope we have such luck today. Are you sure you want to do this?"

"Absolutely." He nodded and sipped his coffee. "Timmy thinks I've lost my mind, but that's beside the point."

"He could be right, you know," she said. "I'm going to put a lot of miles on those long legs of yours."

"I'll tough up. By the way, did you shrink?"

"It's the flat shoes." She lifted a foot from beneath the table for his inspection.

"I see," he said slowly, his gaze roaming lazily over her leg and up to her shapely thigh.

"You have a nice body too," she said, leaning over and peering under the table.

Kellen put his head back and roared with laughter. "Touché," he said. "I consider myself put in my place as an evil, leering man. I can see I'm going to have to be on my toes today. You have a gleam in those beautiful brown eyes of yours."

"Don't mess with me, mister," she said, squinting at him, which brought another whoop of merriment from Kellen.

"Let's go shopping," he said, shaking his head, "before you go completely wacky."

"I have to call Paul and let him know I won't be in." She got up from the table and walked into the living room.

"Wonderful," Kellen muttered, draining his coffee mug and setting it back down with a solid thud.

"Hi, Paul," Paige said into the phone after Paul had picked up on the other end. "I'm just reporting in. I'll be out all day with—on the Kellen Davis job."

"Want to meet for lunch?" Paul asked.

"No, I, uh, really don't know where I'll be. Stocks are depleted at this time of year, you know, and . . . well, wish me luck."

"Don't worry about it," Paul growled. "If we don't make the hot-shot's deadline, it's no biggy."

"Yes, well, I've got to run."

"Paige, are you all right? You don't sound like yourself."

"I'm fine, just in a rush. Bye, Paul."

"Good-bye."

As Paige replaced the receiver she turned to see Kellen leaning against the doorjamb to the kitchen, his arms folded loosely over his chest.

"Why didn't you tell him I was going with you?" he asked. "Wouldn't he approve?"

"It's not unusual for a client to accompany me on a shopping trip. Paul would have no objection."

"But you didn't mention I was along for the ride today."

"It didn't seem necessary."

"Or you preferred he be kept in the dark," Kellen said, frowning.

"Meaning?"

"I don't know, you tell me. I somehow get the feeling that Paul Martin plays a very important role in your life."

"Of course he does," she said, her voice rising slightly. "He's my employer and a very good friend. But what gives you the right to question my relationship with him?"

"The same right you had to pin me to the wall about Hildy Holt and Felicia Evans. The fact that we care who and what is going on in each other's lives is important here. Dammit, Paige," he bellowed, "is there something between you and that flaky decorator or not?"

Paige opened her mouth, shut it, opened it again, and suddenly burst into laughter. Holding her stomach, she sank onto the sofa, gasping for breath. Kellen moved toward her cautiously, obviously surprised at her reaction to his outburst.

"Paige?" he said tentatively.

"Oh, I'm sorry," she said, trying to compose herself. "I got carried away."

"What's so damn funny?"

"You. Paul. Men. You're both acting like little boys trying to protect your turf. Which," she added breezily, standing and brushing past him, "neither of you owns in the first place."

"We'll see about *that,*" Kellen muttered under his breath.

The air was crisp and the sky a clear blue as they

drove to the first store on Paige's list. Kellen was soon caught up in her buoyant mood. He was seeing yet another side of Paige—a happy, carefree, vivacious young woman whose eyes were sparkling—and he was delighted. He was immediately impressed with the respect she was shown by the salespeople in the exclusive shops and admired the way she politely but firmly refused to purchase anything less than exactly what they were looking for. He couldn't remember when he had felt so relaxed, comfortable, ready to smile. Paige's enthusiasm was infectious, and when the first grouping for the living room was completed, he nearly cheered aloud at their success.

Timmy would have him committed, he thought, shaking his head ruefully as he waited for Paige to complete the paperwork on a set of lamps they had chosen. Kellen Davis, superstar, getting excited over sofas and throw pillows. Brother. And Paige was so different today. The tightness, the wariness, were gone. Was she beginning to trust him? Had last night helped bring about this change? She had felt good in his arms, and he'd wanted to make love to her so badly—but he would have blown it. She wasn't ready for that step yet. Lord, what if she never was? Kellen wondered. He'd go out of his mind! He'd—

"All set," she said to him cheerfully. "I arranged for delivery. How about some lunch, Mr. Client? I'm buying."

"On your expense account?"

"You bet."

"Let's go," he said. Score one for me, Paul old buddy. The House of Martin was about to spring for the most expensive thing on the menu, Kellen thought, a smug look on his face as he circled Paige's shoulders with his arm and hurried her out of the store.

The afternoon was a repeat performance of the

morning as Paige literally dragged Kellen through endless stores in search of the precise furniture they wanted. They argued loudly over a chair that Kellen declared too small for even a little old lady, while Paige retorted that he didn't have to sit in it then, for heaven's sake. He refused to change his mind, and she rolled her eyes and stomped off to find something else. They settled on a Queen Anne chair with footstool, covered in chocolate-brown velvet, and shook hands in agreement, grinning at each other.

At five o'clock Paige sank onto an overstuffed silk brocade love seat in a showroom in Scottsdale and sighed deeply. "I'm exhausted," she said. "That's it for today."

"I'm just getting warmed up," Kellen said, rubbing his hands together eagerly. "Let's go buy some books."

"No-o-o," she moaned.

"You mean, we're finished?"

"Absolutely, positively, yes!"

"Well, darn. Hey, I'm hungry. Let's go out to my house and send out for pizza."

"I—"

"Oh my," a woman suddenly exclaimed, rushing up to Kellen, "you're Kellen Davis."

"I am?" he said, smiling at the wide-eyed woman.

"Could—could I . . ." she stammered. "I mean . . . if you don't mind . . . uh . . . Mr. Davis, may I have your autograph?"

"Certainly."

"I know I have a paper and pen in here," the woman said, rummaging through her purse. "I'm so thrilled about this. Oh, Martha, come over here quickly, dear. This is Kellen Davis, the movie star!"

Paige watched in wonder as the exuberant fan's voice boomed over the expanse of the store, causing heads to snap up in attention. Like bees swarming to a field of wild flowers, shoppers and clerks descended on Kellen in excited animation. They pressed against him, jostling for position to get his signature on scraps of paper, shopping bags, anything they could find. Paige slipped off the love seat and worked her way to the back of the crowd. She saw Kellen's dazzling smile as he signed his name over and over. He winked seductively at a shapely blond girl who insisted he sign her upper arm. He offered no resistance when another young woman ran her hand over his chest, and he bent over to say something to her that caused her to giggle and quickly pull away.

A wave of disgust swept through Paige as she turned and hurried to the door of the store and out onto the sidewalk. She leaned against the building, taking a deep breath before sinking onto a bench near the curb.

They were hanging all over him, she thought with disgust, pawing him, and he was loving every minute of it. She had felt so comfortable with Kellen today. They had laughed, talked, shared, and she'd forgotten who he really was. But that was what was wrong here. She didn't know which of his personalities was real. Had he been acting out a role during these hours they'd been together? How gullible she was to believe that the great Kellen Davis was actually excited about furniture, for heaven's sake. What did he want from her? Why was he playing this game? She must get away from here, go home and—

"Quick," Kellen said, suddenly appearing beside her and grabbing her arm, "let's go before they trap me again."

Before Paige could reply, she was literally lifted off her perch and propelled along the sidewalk and around the corner to where the car was parked. Kellen all but pushed her into the front seat and ran around to the driver's side. He slid behind the wheel and roared the car into action.

"Kellen, what—"

"Made it," he said, glancing in the rearview mirror as he pulled onto the street. "Ready for that pizza?"

"I'm tired, Kellen. I think I'll just go on home," Paige said quietly.

"Hey, what's wrong? You look as though you lost your best friend. Do you feel all right? Wait a minute here. You're upset about what happened in the store with those women, aren't you? I couldn't help it, Paige, they came out of nowhere and—"

"You didn't exactly hate it," she said, her voice tight. "It would make my skin crawl to have strangers touch me like that, but you certainly—"

"That's enough!" he said angrily. "You are passing judgment on something you know absolutely nothing about."

"You bet I don't and I have no desire to find out! Who are you, Kellen? Which one of the men I've seen you become is the real person, or do you even know? You push a button and change into anyone that suits your mood. Today when we were together, I thought— But now I see that drooling women are more to your liking than dull hours tromping through furniture stores."

"Oh, man," he growled, smacking the palm of his hand against the steering wheel.

"Take me home," she said, staring out the side window.

"Like hell I will," he roared. "We're going to have this out."

"I am not going to your house."

"Yes, you are! And you're not leaving until we get a few things straight," he said, his jaw clenched tightly.

"This is kidnapping," she shrieked, turning to him in fury.

"Call it what you want, Miss Hoity-toity, but you're coming with me."

"You are a . . . a . . . nerd!"

"Whatever." He shrugged, a sudden grin crossing his face. "Is that the best you could come up with? Nerd?"

"You just shut up, Kellen Davis," she hollered.

He laughed. "You are a mean, scary lady."

"Kellen, I'm warning you, I—"

"Home sweet home," he said, pulling up in front of his wide front porch and turning off the ignition.

"I'm not getting out of this car," she said primly, crossing her arms over her breasts.

"I believe in being fair, so I'll give you a choice. You can walk into the house on your own steam or be carried like a sack of potatoes. Take your pick."

"You wouldn't dare!"

"Try me," he said, getting out, walking around to her door, and opening it.

Paige looked up at the determined expression on Kellen's face and, when she saw the muscle twitch in his tightly set jaw, she scrambled out of the car and ran up the steps ahead of him. She glared at him as he inserted his key and motioned her inside. Kellen strode across the entry hall and into the living room, where he squatted down in front of the hearth and busied himself setting a roaring fire. Paige paced the floor behind him, absolutely seething over his arrogant behavior.

"Now," he said, rising and turning to face her, "we talk."

"No, Kellen, there is nothing—"

"Sit!" he said, pointing to one of the lounge chairs.

"Quit telling me what to do!"

"Okay, stand," he said, lowering himself onto one of the cushioned recliners.

"You are infuriating," she muttered, flopping down in the chair next to him.

"That's beside the point. The issue here is what happened with those women in the store, my reaction to them, and above all, your distorted view of what took place. You are way off base in your evaluation of the crime of which I have been unjustly accused," he said, covering his heart dramatically with his hand.

"Ha!"

"Paige, please listen to me." His voice was suddenly low and serious. "In a way, I'm glad that happened today. You saw a part of my life that is there, and I can't change it. I'm a commodity. I sell myself every time I make a movie and ask people to spend their hard-earned money to see it. In return they're entertained for a couple of hours. Part of the package is that I have to maintain a certain image for those fans when they approach me in public. Kellen Davis, the star, is supposed to be a sex symbol, remember? My responsibility is to maintain that facade when I'm on display. Over the years I've perfected my little show of machismo to the point where I can escape as quickly as possible without being rude. Those women were satisfied, and I wasn't with them for more than ten minutes. Paige, the time I spent with you today was terrific. I truly enjoyed being with you, and I know that once that furniture is here in my home, I'll think of you whenever I look at it."

"Kellen—"

"Let me finish. I realize we come from very different worlds, but that doesn't frighten me. When I'm with you, I'm Kellen Davis, the man, nothing more or less. I will never perform for you, Paige, or be something

I'm not. I'm being completely honest with you, and that's the best I have to offer."

Paige pushed herself to her feet and walked to the fireplace. She stared into the leaping flames for several minutes before turning to face Kellen. "I'm sorry," she said softly. "I behaved like a child and I apologize. I was very unfair to you. Please forgive me, Kellen."

"Oh, babe." He walked over to her and gripped her shoulders. "Don't you see? We can't change what happens in the world when we step outside, but we can leave it out there. Give us a chance to discover what we might be to each other in our private space."

A warmth shone in Kellen's sapphire-blue eyes as he slowly lowered his head and with a gentle, tender kiss claimed Paige's mouth. As if she were made of the most fragile china, he gathered her close to him, placing fluttering kisses over her face and down her slender throat. The motion was as light as a butterfly's wing, but it sent a surge of desire through Paige, and she leaned against him, wrapping her arms around his neck. Still he kissed her with maddening restraint until she could bear it no longer. With a soft moan she buried her hands in his thick hair and pulled him to her, pressing her mouth onto his.

He responded immediately, his control vanishing as he explored the dark inner regions of her mouth with his tongue. His strong hands slid down over her hips, molding them to his as she rose on tiptoe to arch against him. She felt his male desire pressing against her as his fingertips inched up the hem of her sweater. He gently caressed her aching breasts, which responded instantly to his touch. His lips never leaving hers, he lowered her to the plush carpet. In the glow from the fire she could see the smoldering desire reflected in his eyes as he gazed down at her passion-flushed face.

"I want you, Paige," he said, his voice raspy, "but I can't read your mind. Whatever you decide will be how it will go. I told you once I'd never take anything from you that you weren't prepared to give. I meant that."

She wanted him so much, she thought. Now. This minute. She had said these hours would be theirs. But what would become of her if she gave herself totally to this man? She had enjoyed every moment of their time together, but if she passed into his care, the very essence of her being would be lost. Kellen had invoked passions within her she didn't know she possessed. What if she came to love him? He might never love her in return and— "Kellen, I—I can't."

"Enough said." He smiled and kissed her quickly.

"You must think I'm a tease, a—"

"You are, Paige Cunningham—the kind who makes me laugh right out loud. You are the one who makes me so damn angry, I could paddle that cute little tush of yours. You are the one who makes me forget the madness I work in and remember who I really am. You are . . . my lady."

For how long? Paige thought, shivering slightly. Oh, Kellen, for how long?

Kellen pushed himself to his feet and extended his hand to Paige, who rose to stand by his side. He pulled her gently to him and held her, stroking her hair. She closed her eyes for a moment, took a steadying breath, and then looked up at Kellen. He was smiling tenderly at her.

Four

"You're gorgeous," Kellen said, kissing her on the end of her nose. "It'll take too long for a pizza to be delivered out here. Let's raid the refrigerator."

"Lead on," she said, following him into the kitchen.

It was fun. They laughed and talked and created an enormous omelet that boasted a vast array of ingredients they tossed into it, using a variety of leftovers they found in the fridge. They made a tower of hot, buttery toast and a pot of steaming coffee and devoured every bite of the offering. Together they cleaned up the kitchen, Kellen holding the dustpan when Paige swept the floor.

With one more mug of coffee they settled in front of the fireplace in the living room, pulling the lounge chairs close together and staring into the flames as they sat in comfortable silence.

"I'll never forget today, Paige," Kellen said finally, his voice low.

"It was wonderful," she whispered, smiling at him. "I can't remember when I've felt so . . . so alive and happy."

"You should always be that way."

"That isn't very realistic," she said, frowning slightly. "No one goes around with a continual smile on his face."

"That's true, but there should be more joy than pain. Sometimes it takes a little work to tip the scales in the proper direction."

"Are you content with your life, Kellen?"

"Most of the time. I'm usually so busy, I hardly have an opportunity to dwell on it, especially now that I've started my own production company. Every once in a while, though, I get rather lonely."

"That seems impossible," she said, shaking her head. "You're constantly surrounded by people, excitement, a fast-paced existence that never stops."

"But there is that hour of the day when you close the door on it all. Sometimes the peace and quiet is heavenly, and other nights . . . Well, I'd like to have someone to sit in front of the fire with and talk to. I guess what I'm saying is that I'm very glad you're here with me, Paige." He reached for her hand and lifted it to his lips.

"I really should be getting home," she said. A tingling sensation was spreading through her at the touch of his sensuous lips on the palm of her hand.

"Not yet. Stay a while longer. I have one day before everything breaks loose on the picture. Let's share it. All of it. Stay, Paige."

"Yes, Kellen," she said, her voice a hushed whisper. "I want to be here with you for the hours we have left before your world claims you again."

"Don't make it sound so final, like it will all be over when we actually start shooting."

"We'll see," she said softly. "We'll see."

He squeezed her hand. "I'm glad I found you, Paige. We're going to have the greatest Christmas together and—"

"Kellen, please, no talk of tomorrow. Goodness, I'm so sleepy. That fire is hypnotizing me."

"Then close your eyes, pretty Paige."

"Just for a moment." She closed her eyes, relaxing into the cushions of the lounge chair.

"Sweet dreams," he whispered.

The dream crept in on her and she struggled against it, trying to chase the vivid pictures from her mind. Snow was falling so thickly that heavy drifts were created immediately, making it difficult to move as she tried to push her way forward. Jerry ran on ahead, leaping over the icy obstacles and laughing back at her over his shoulder. She cried out to him in vain, then stumbled and fell. The snow covered her, burying her beneath a crushing weight, and she screamed in fear.

"Paige! Wake up!" Kellen said, shaking her gently by the shoulders.

"No! Jerry, no! Don't go out there! No!"

"Paige!"

"What?" she whispered, blinking her eyes. "Oh, Kellen, Kellen," she sobbed, wrapping her arms around his neck.

"It's okay, babe, I'm here. You had a nightmare."

"I'm sorry. I . . ."

"Shhh. You're trembling, Paige. Take a deep breath and try to relax."

"I'm all right now."

"Was Jerry your husband?" he asked gently.

"Yes. Did I call his name? Oh, Kellen, forgive me. I never meant to bring him into our—"

"When did he die?"

"It will be two years ago, on Christmas Eve."

"Christmas . . . my God," he whispered. "I had no

idea. No wonder you don't like the holiday season. What happened, Paige? Was it an accident?"

"He was skiing. We were in Aspen," she said, her voice low and flat. "I didn't want to go. I thought we'd celebrate Christmas in our little house in Denver, but Jerry insisted that we travel to— Oh, please, Kellen, I don't want to talk about this."

"All right, Paige. Can I get you something? A brandy?"

"No. I'm fine. I am so very sorry, Kellen. I feel foolish about screaming in my sleep like a child. It's just that sometimes I have nightmares that—"

"Enough. I'll hold you right here in my arms," he said, moving his chair next to hers and pulling her into his arms.

"Thank you," she said wearily, snuggling close to him.

Kellen frowned as he held her tightly. His poor, precious Paige, he thought. Now her aversion to Christmas made sense. She wouldn't be alone during the holidays, not this time. He was going to be with her every spare minute he had. He'd protect her from her ghosts and help her learn to laugh again. She'd been dealt a lousy hand and she deserved so much better. He'd make her happy; he swore he would. Somehow. He never wanted her to be hurt again by anyone or anything. He wouldn't allow it to happen. Paige Cunningham was not going to cry any more tears of sorrow. She was *his* lady.

Paige dozed again for a short time and then opened her eyes, relishing the feel of being held in Kellen's arms. Suddenly she remembered the nightmare, the haunting picture of Jerry's laughing face, and Kellen's comforting words.

Oh, no, she thought, why did that have to happen? Why had Jerry walked from the past into her present? Damn you, Jerry Cunningham. All she wanted was a small piece of happiness with Kellen. Jerry had to leave her be!

"Hello, sleepy girl," Kellen said.

"Gosh, I'm fun company, aren't I?" She laughed shakily. "I am definitely going home."

"And get a good night's rest so we can go shopping again tomorrow. I'm really getting into this decorating stuff, you know. I've already got the frowning and nodding down pat. How would it be if I sort of stroked my chin and squinted when I'm looking at a chair?"

"Perfect. The owners of the shops will be very impressed."

At Paige's apartment Kellen kissed her deeply and then trailed his thumb gently over her lips before turning to leave.

"I'll see you in the morning," he said.

"Good night, Kellen."

Once in bed, Paige fell asleep instantly, not waking until dawn. No haunting nightmares marred her peaceful slumber. She was smiling when she opened the door to Kellen, who immediately pulled her into his arms and claimed her mouth in a long, searing kiss.

"Sorry I'm late," he said when he finally released her, "but Timmy called."

"What did he want?" she asked, taking a steadying breath.

"Who?"

"Timmy!"

"Oh, he said Felicia is flying in this afternoon and wants us all to go out to dinner. You taste so good."

He reached for her again, but Paige sidestepped him.

"Felicia Evans is arriving in Phoenix today?" she asked, frowning.

"Yep. You'll like her. She plays very sultry, sophisticated roles, but in actuality she's down-to-earth and has a great sense of humor. You'll see for yourself when you meet her tonight."

"Me?"

"Sure. I told Timmy to make reservations for four. He can pick up Felicia and we'll join them. You do want to go, don't you?"

"I . . . I'm not . . ."

"It'll be fun. Come here, pretty Paige, and let me say another good morning to you."

"Kellen, about tonight. I— Oh!" She gasped as his lips silenced her and then trailed down the slender column of her neck.

"Oh, Paige," Kellen whispered, a shudder sweeping through his body.

"Kellen, what's wrong?"

He tightened his arms around her. "I . . . damn."

"Kellen?"

"Paige, you . . . we . . . together we experience something incredible. You're stirring up strange, unexpected emotions in me. I don't mind telling you, lady, you scare the hell out of me."

"I'm not sure I understand."

"It doesn't matter if you do, I guess. Just believe me when I say I've never known anyone like you before and I'm very, very glad you came into my life."

She nuzzled her face in his neck. "This is where I belong, Kellen, for now. You've given me so much. I feel alive and feminine and blissfully young. Everything we've shared is like a precious gem, a private treasure known only to ourselves. I'll cherish these memories forever."

He pulled back slightly so he could look into her face. "You're doing it again, Paige," he said. "You're making it sound like what we have is over before it even begins."

She buried her face again and tightened her hold

on him. "Don't, Kellen. We have to be realistic. You're about to step back into your world and I'll return to mine. We have today to enjoy but then—"

"Dammit, Paige, it isn't going to end just because—"

"Kellen, let's not argue. I feel so wonderful right now. Don't spoil this moment."

"Will you go to dinner tonight?"

"I . . . yes, all right."

"Okay. I'll settle for that much for the time being. Now!" He stepped back from her. "We've got to hit the stores. I'm tired of furniture. Let's buy books!"

"But what about the rest of the living room?"

"You can do it. Pick whatever you like. I'm itching to fill those shelves."

She laughed. "You're spoiled."

"I know. I'm big on getting what I want. Consider that fair warning. Come on!"

While Kellen scowled Paige telephoned Paul and informed him that she would once again be busy the entire day purchasing items for Kellen's home. Bidding Paul a hasty good-bye, she hung up before he could voice the objection she knew he was all too eager to deliver.

She and Kellen first stopped at a quaint little store that sold both new and used books. Kellen's eyes were sparkling as he roamed through the narrow stacks. "Fantastic," he said. "Look, Paige, here are all the classics. Shakespeare, Mark Twain, Hemingway, everything."

"You enjoy those?" she asked, her eyes widening in surprise.

"Sure. And mysteries. I'll want all the Agatha Christies and— Hey, here's a history of the Old West."

"I'll tell the clerk to get some boxes."

For the next two hours they steadily filled the cartons that had been provided. Paige was impressed by the wide variety of reading material Kellen wished to have in his home. More than once he picked up a thick novel and told her the plot, often reciting passages from memory.

"When do you find time to read?" she asked finally.

"I'm not doing my macho thing every minute, you know," he said indignantly.

"Could have fooled me," she said, her gaze raking over his massive frame.

"No free looks, lady," he said, shoving a book into her hands.

"Aw, shucks."

With the help of the stock boy the books were loaded into the trunk of the car. Kellen patted it when they were done, nodding his head in satisfaction.

"I'll be right back," he said, after opening the car door for Paige.

She watched curiously as he dashed back into the store and emerged a few minutes later with a gift-wrapped package under his arm. He made no reference to his purchase and simply placed it on the seat between them.

"I have an idea," he said as he turned the key in the ignition. "It's warm enough in the sun to eat outside. Let's pick up some hamburgers and go over to Encanto Park."

"You're hungry again?"

"Of course. I signed fifteen autographs for that saleswoman in the bookstore. Do you believe she really has that many granddaughters? Anyway, I'd sure like a peaceful lunch."

"Then a picnic it is," Paige said.

An hour later they were settled on a park bench munching on hamburgers and French fries, and drinking thick milk shakes. Kellen grinned when a large white duck waddled out of the water and took a fry from Kellen's fingers.

"Now, that's a great duck," he said. "Tell me, Paige, have you ever seen such a super duck?"

"Oh, Kellen." She laughed. "You continually amaze me. You get such pleasure out of simple things. It's a wonderful trait. You make me stop and appreciate so much that I haven't given thought to before."

"That's a good lead-in to my next line," he said, looking at her intently as he picked up the package he had bought in the book store. "I got this for you. No, for us. We'll share it."

"I know it must be a book, but why are you being so serious?"

"Because I don't want to upset you," he said, slowly tearing away the gift wrapping. "But, Paige, I really feel that in order to have a future you must bury the past. This book is about Christmas and—"

"Kellen, no."

"Listen to me," he said, placing the leatherbound volume on her lap. "Christmas isn't a time of death. It's a story of a birth, a new life. It's celebrated all over the world. That's what this book is about. It tells of the ways the holiday is marked in different lands. We're going to read it together, word by word. The customs and costumes and traditions may be different, but one thing is constant. It's a joyous time everywhere. That's what we're going to do, Paige, bring the happiness back into your Christmas."

"Kellen, I . . . oh, Kellen." She covered her face with her hands as uncontrollable tears spilled over onto her cheeks.

"Come here," he said gently, pulling her close and holding her tightly. "I knew you'd cry, but we've got to start somewhere. Dry your tears and then we'll look at the book."

"Why are you doing this?" she said between sobs. "It's cruel. Every tree, every carol, every Santa Claus reminds me of— No, Kellen, I won't be tormented like this!"

"Yes!" He grabbed her by the shoulders and shook her slightly. "You owe it to yourself. It's been two years since your husband died, and you still allow this season to rake you over emotional coals. Enough is enough. I'm sure you loved him very much, and I understand that the anniversary of his death is an especially difficult time. But, Paige, you had to have been the most important thing in that man's life and he wouldn't want you to destroy the joys of—"

"No!" she shrieked, pulling out of Kellen's arms and stumbling to her feet. "You don't understand anything about it. Jerry didn't love me, Kellen!"

"What are you saying?" he said, getting up and turning her to face him.

"He— Oh, God, I can't do this," she said, a sob catching in her throat.

"Talk to me, Paige." Kellen carefully sat her back down on the bench.

"Jerry was a carefree, happy man," she said softly, clutching her hands tightly in her lap. "No, he was a boy, really. He never grew up. Everything was a game to him, an adventure. When my parents died while I was in college, I was so alone. Jerry was like a ray of sunshine in my life. I met him about a year after I graduated. He was an architect, and the firm I was working for had been hired to decorate an office building he'd designed. I— Kellen, please . . ."

"Go on," he said quietly, covering her hands with his.

"He dated a lot of women and I enjoyed his company too. He was always coming up with exciting, unexpected things to do. I was also seeing a professor at the college, and Jerry was insanely jealous about that, but we had no commitment so . . . Then Jerry asked me to marry him. I was shocked. I mean, he didn't seem like the type to settle down. I was swept off my feet and a week later I was Mrs. Cunningham and deliriously happy. A few months later I learned the truth."

"About what?"

"Jerry bragged about it one night when he was drunk. He had gone to see the professor and warned him to stay away from me. The professor showed him an engagement ring he had bought and said he intended to propose to me. Jerry was livid. That awful night he told me how he had beat the other guy at his own game and snatched up the prize first. He never loved me, Kellen; he just couldn't stand the thought of losing out on a trophy."

"My God," Kellen whispered, a muscle tightening in his jaw.

"I thought I could make him learn to love me, but I was nothing more than a possession. That last Christmas we'd been married for three years, and it was going to be my final attempt to make our marriage work. Jerry had always insisted we travel during the holidays, flitting from one place to another, but that year I planned a quiet dinner and bought a little tree and . . . well, Jerry came bursting in the door and said we were going to Aspen with a crowd. I pleaded with him to stay home, but he said he'd go without me."

"So you went?"

"Yes," she said, sighing deeply. "I didn't want to be alone on Christmas. I had done that too often after my parents died. Aspen was a nightmare."

"What happened, Paige?"

"The professor was there, with his new wife. Jerry was horrible. He had been drinking and he kept taunting the man about me right in front of his wife. I couldn't stand it anymore. I screamed at Jerry to stop. I told him we were finished and I was getting a divorce. Everyone in the place was staring at us and I ran out of the inn. Jerry was furious and in a fit of temper took off for the ski slopes. He was too drunk to navigate turns and . . . and . . ."

"That was when he died?"

"Yes." Her voice was hardly above a whisper. "I never should have said those things to him in public. I drove him to do something reckless that cost him his life. I killed my husband, Kellen."

"No! My God, no, you didn't!" Kellen said fiercely, pulling her into his arms. "The man was a fool not to love you and bless the day you agreed to marry him. He didn't deserve you, Paige. What happened to him he brought on himself. Dammit, Paige, don't let him cause you pain from the grave. He hurt you enough while he was alive."

"Oh, Kellen, I've gone over that scene in the inn a thousand times in my mind. I see myself leaving the room; Jerry follows me, and then we talk privately. But I announced to the world that Jerry Cunningham had lost, and he couldn't handle that. I brought his body back to Denver on Christmas Day. Everywhere I looked I saw smiling people and decorations, and it all seemed to be taunting me. I thought I had recovered, but last Christmas it all came rushing back. I went on a cruise over the holidays and the whole ship looked like the North Pole. I've never seen so many trees and Santas. Jerry's face seemed to be reflected in every ornament, laughing at me, letting me know I'd never be free of the memories."

"You will be," Kellen said, gently stroking her hair. "I promise you that, Paige. But you've got to trust me."

"Don't take on my ghosts, Kellen. They'll only drag you down."

"I'll be the judge of that."

"No, Kellen, I don't want—"

Paige's words were silenced by Kellen's lips claiming hers in a soft kiss that intensified almost immediately as he gathered her tightly against him. He could feel the tears on her cheeks and the trembling in her slender body as she circled his neck with her arms and received the warmth of his caress. When he at last lifted his head, he cupped her face in his large hands and brushed the moisture from her eyes with his thumbs.

"You won't cry again," he said, "not for him or the past. I'm taking you to my house now, Paige. We have a book to read. Together."

Paige allowed Kellen to grasp her hand and lead her from the park. She felt like an obedient child, unable to muster the energy to protest as he helped her into the car. She was emotionally drained and closed her eyes as she leaned her head back on the top of the seat.

She'd ruined everything, she thought miserably. She'd destroyed the lovely place she and Kellen had created for themselves. She hadn't wanted Kellen to know about Jerry and the things that had happened. She and Kellen had come so far, so quickly. They had talked, laughed, and shared, and he had brought an aura of contentment to her life she would have never dreamed possible. He seemed to be reaching out to her, asking her to trust and believe in him, and she wanted to. They might come to have so much together if— But she knew Kellen was only feeling a momentary wave of pity for her. He'd be glad to be rid of her with her tears and hang-ups.

"Are you awake?" Kellen asked, placing his hand on her cheek. "We're home."

We're home? she thought, opening her eyes and looking at him in surprise. What an insane thing to say. He made it sound as if *they* lived here. Welcome to Paige and Kellen's house. Come right in . . .

"Paige?"

"I'm sorry, Kellen. I'm not myself. Maybe it would be best if you took me to my apartment."

"No, I'm not leaving you alone. I forced you to drag up painful memories and tell me about them, and you're staying here for a while. Let's go in. I think you should rest and—"

"Kellen, stop treating me like a child," she snapped angrily. "You're hovering over me as though I were going to have a complete mental breakdown in the next five minutes. Before I told you about Jerry, you saw me as a woman. Now I'm a pathetic creature who needs a nap to settle her jangled nerves. I can take care of myself, Kellen Davis, and absolutely do not need a nursemaid!"

"Now that you've gotten your tantrum out of the way, do you think you could get out of the car?" he asked calmly.

"Of course," she said primly. She did so, and stomped up the stairs to the front door.

Inside the house Kellen slammed the door shut and grabbed Paige by the arm. He pushed her back against the door, placing one large hand on either side of her head. She looked up at him in shock at his abrupt action, her eyes widening as she saw the stormy expression on his face.

"To me," he growled, "you are still a very beautiful, very desirable woman. How dare you insult me by saying I'd change my feelings for you because your husband was a bum. That is the dumbest thing I have ever heard! Some of the women in my past were no prize packages either! What's important is now! Have you got that? Well?"

"I . . . yes, I guess so," she said, her head bobbing up and down.

"Good! March yourself upstairs and go to bed!"

"I will not!" she said, planting her hands on her hips.

"That's it! I've had it!" He scooped her into his arms and marched up the stairs.

"Dammit, Kellen, put me down," she yelled.

"Tsk, tsk. Such language." He chuckled as he entered the bedroom and tossed her unceremoniously onto the bed.

"I told you I am not a child! I am a—"

"Woman," he said softly, moving quickly and covering her body with his massive frame. "A passionate, fantastic woman."

"Oh, Kellen," she whispered, "I can't think straight when you—"

Kellen kissed her so softly, so gently that Paige had to blink back the tears that stung her eyes. Every muscle in his body was taut, coiled; he held himself in check as his tongue sought and found hers. Paige felt herself relax under his soothing caresses and welcomed the now familiar desire that was surging through her body.

He was doing this for her. He was kissing away her pain and grief, bringing her back to the world she shared only with him. She felt him tremble slightly and realized instantly what it was costing him to maintain his control. Was she really this important to Kellen? Was it possible that they might come to have more than just a fleeting glimpse of happiness together?

"So nice," he murmured, moving away and pulling her close.

"Yes." She smiled and brushed a thick lock of his hair off his forehead. "Oh, yes."

"I'm tired," he said, nibbling on her ear. "Let's take a nap."

She knew what he was doing. He was convinced she needed to rest after that emotional scene in the park and he was pretending to be tired. He was so dear, she thought dreamily. She wasn't going to argue about it. She *was* sleepy. She'd just close her eyes and . . .

"Sweet dreams," Kellen whispered, kissing her gently on the forehead after pulling the bedspread over her. "No more painful memories, my sweet."

Moving carefully so as not to disturb Paige, Kellen edged off the bed. For the next hour he busied himself unloading the books from the car and placing them on the shelves in the living room. Satisfied with his work, he built a roaring fire in the hearth and sat in a lounge chair, staring into the flames as he sipped a cup of coffee.

Okay, Davis, he thought, a frown on his face, *you've run out of little chores to keep you busy; it's time to sort some things out.* Paige's story about that louse of a husband of hers was incredible. The man must have been insane not to love her, to treat her like a precious, wonderful gift. She'd been through hell, but that was all over now. Things were going to be different because he was there to make sure that . . . that what? What did he have to offer her? A merry Christmas? Yeah, he'd do that, come hell or high water, but then? He wanted to make love to her so much, but . . .

In a frustrated gesture Kellen got to his feet and began to pace the floor restlessly. He raked his hand through his hair and his glance fell on the leather-bound book about Christmas in countries around the world. He was soon lost in the beautiful pictures and narratives and much later snapped the book shut with a determined expression on his face. He bounded up the stairs two at a time, then slowed his pace as he entered his bedroom.

Paige was sleeping peacefully, her dark hair spread out over the pillow in a soft halo. Kellen gazed at her, his heart quickening as her thick eyelashes fluttered. Then she opened her eyes and smiled at him.

"Hello, Mr. Davis," she said quietly.

"Hello, pretty lady. May I join you?"

"Of course. I see you intend to read in bed."

"Will you look at the book?" he asked, a concerned expression on his face.

"Yes, Kellen. We'll share it together."

Did he deserve this much trust from her? he thought suddenly. Could he guarantee that he wouldn't hurt her?

"Kellen?"

"Move over," he said with a smile. "It's Show-and-Tell time."

Propped up against the large pillows, they slowly read the enchanting book, commenting often on the beautiful pictures.

"Hey, let's go to Mexico so I can take a swing at one of those piñatas," Kellen said, his eyes shining.

"Oh, Kellen, look at this Advent wreath they have in Germany. Those pastries look scrumptious! And, my goodness, in Puerto Rico the children set out boxes of grass for the Wise Men's camels instead of hanging stockings for Santa Claus. . . ."

An hour later Kellen slowly closed the book and kissed Paige on the top of her head. She smiled up at him, picked up the volume, and held it tightly to her breasts.

"One thing is the same in every land," Kellen said softly. "It is a joyous time, cause for celebration and happiness. That's what I want for you this holiday season, Paige."

"I know you do and I thank you so much. Sitting here with you like this, seeing these beautiful pictures, I can't imagine it being any other way. Kellen, you are the only person that I've told about what happened in Aspen that year. Perhaps I'll be able to deal with it now that I've brought it to the surface, but I don't want to do anything to spoil your Christmas."

"Paige, we'll take it one step at a time. Everything will be fine, you'll see. Now! Come and check out what I've done to the bookshelves. I did a superior job!"

"I thought *I* was the decorator."

"I'm in training. If my fans desert me, I'll need something to fall back on."

The telephone was ringing just as they reached the bottom of the stairs, and Kellen answered it quickly, a wide smile immediately spreading over his face. "Hello yourself, gorgeous," he said. "How have you been?"

Paige walked to the fireplace and tried to concentrate on examining the books Kellen had placed on the shelves. She could hear his deep, throaty laughter and was painfully aware of the endearments—*darling*, *honey*, and *sweetheart*—he was delivering to the person on the other end of the line.

"Great," he said finally. "See you then."

"Somehow I feel that wasn't Timmy," Paige said, forcing a smile as Kellen hung up the receiver.

"Nope, it was Felicia. She just checked into the Camelback Inn. She's looking forward to going out to dinner tonight."

"Maybe she'd prefer to catch up on old times. I really don't have to go along, Kellen. I'm sure Felicia would—"

"Love to meet you," he interrupted, crossing the room to her. "I'll get dressed here, and then we'll go to your place so you can change. It's going to be a great evening. So what do you think of my books? Not bad, huh?"

Felicia Evans, Paige thought wildly. What was she doing with these people? They were two of the most popular stars in Hollywood, and she was calmly tagging along for dinner as though she fit in with their jet-setting crowd. She and Kellen had created a private world, and now they must open the doors and allow all to enter. She didn't belong here.

"Paige?"

"What? Oh. The shelves are splendid, Kellen. Of course, you need much more on them but it's a fine start."

"*I* thought so." He nodded proudly.

"I should call Paul."

"Why?"

"To report in. I can't just disappear for an entire day. It's late. He may have left the office already."

"I certainly hope so," Kellen muttered under his breath.

No one answered at the House of Martin, and Paige replaced the receiver slowly, a frown on her face. "He's not going to be very happy that I didn't contact him earlier," she said. "I'll phone first thing in the morning before I go shopping for you again."

"He'll live. Hey, get me a TV, okay? I like to catch the late news."

"Yes, sir."

"We, pretty person, are going to have a fantastic time tonight. Felicia is great. We'll . . ."

Paige listened absently, pretending to be enthusiastic about the coming hours but unable to brush aside the icy misery that had clutched her. To Kellen the evening was just another sparkling outing on the town. To her it meant only one thing: The fantasy was over, the bubble had burst, and she had to give Kellen back to the world where he really belonged.

Tonight would mean good-bye.

Five

Wrapped in a fluffy towel after her shower, Paige viewed the selection of clothes in her closet. Through the half-closed bedroom door she could hear the murmur of voices from the television Kellen had switched on to watch while he waited for her to change for dinner.

There was no backing out now, and she reached for the dress in her wardrobe that would give her courage: a bright cranberry-colored challis. The neckline was low, cut to show the tops of her full breasts, and the fabric fell in soft folds from the shoulders. She slid it over her head, then examined how it clung to her small waist and molded to the gentle slopes of her hips. It was, she decided, a very sexy dress and just what she needed to brazen her way through an evening in the company of Felicia Evans. Paige had seen photographs of the red-haired actress and knew that Felicia was extraordinarily beautiful and had a voluptuous figure. Never married, the star was rumored to have had numerous affairs over the years, usually with the leading man in the films she starred in.

Including Kellen? Paige thought. No, he had said they were like brother and sister. But how could any woman be held in Kellen's arms, kissed and caressed without responding? She didn't care if the cameras were rolling, no one could be immune to the sensations that man stirred up! Felicia would have to be dead not to succumb to Kellen's touch. But he was an actor. He seduced whomever the script said was next on the list, turned on the charm and sex appeal, and bingo! When the scene was over, he walked away. That was Kellen Davis the movie star. In real life he was warm and tender and—honest? He'd been so good to her, so thoughtful and caring. It hadn't been a role he'd been playing, she knew it hadn't! She needed to believe in what they had shared.

"Are you almost ready?" Kellen called.

"Yes, I'm coming," Paige answered, turning around to take one more appraising glance in the mirror. Here goes nothing, she thought, turning off the light and leaving the bedroom.

Good God, Kellen thought, getting to his feet the moment Paige appeared, she was a vision of loveliness. She looked like a doll that should be placed under glass and set on a shelf where nothing could harm her. "Paige," he said quietly, "you are the most beautiful woman I have ever seen."

"Oh, Kellen." She laughed softly. "That's silly. Nice to hear, but definitely farfetched. You hang out in Hollywood, remember? That, kind sir, is the beauty spot of America. Just for fun though, I'll pretend I'm ravishingly gorgeous like you said. Shall we go dazzle the public?"

"We shall." And the first guy that gave her the once-over was going to have a broken jaw, Kellen told himself firmly, helping her on with her coat.

"When Felicia Evans and Kellen Davis step out on the town, how do you avoid the crowds that gather?" Paige asked as they drove to the restaurant.

"Timmy will have made arrangements for a private room at the restaurant."

"Where are we going?"

"El Sombrero. Felicia says she's hungry for Mexican food. I hope that's all right with you."

"Of course." Heaven forbid Felicia shouldn't have what she wanted, Paige thought. Oh, dear, that was *not* nice. She had to work on her attitude about this woman.

To Paige's surprise Kellen drove through the parking lot of the restaurant and around to the back where he parked next to a large trash bin. After helping her out, he gripped her elbow and led her to a door where he knocked solidly three times.

"I feel like a spy," she whispered.

"Tricks of the trade," he said with a chuckle. The door was opened and they entered an enormous kitchen that was bustling with busy people.

"Señor Davis, welcome," a short Mexican man said, pumping Kellen's hand vigorously. "If you will follow me?"

"Thank you," Kellen said. "I appreciate your going to all this trouble."

"We are honored to have you here. Your Mr. Winslow did mention that perhaps you and Miss Evans might be so kind as to sign a few of our menus. Of course, I do not wish to impose. . . ."

Kellen smiled. "It will be a pleasure."

"Splendid." The man beamed. "Come, I will take you to the others. They arrived a few minutes ago. Miss Evans is even more beautiful in person than on the screen. Ah, but this lovely lady with you is also exquisite."

"I know," Kellen said smugly.

"Lord," Paige muttered, feeling her cheeks grow warm.

"Here you are," the man said, bowing in front of a closed door. "A waiter will be in to serve you shortly."

"Thanks," Kellen said, reaching for the handle.

"Kellen, wait," Paige said, placing her hand on his arm. "I—"

"Yes?"

"Why do I suddenly wish I were home watching TV?" she said miserably.

"Oh, babe." He smiled down at her. "Just relax. You know Timmy, and Felicia is no different from your next-door neighbor."

"I can't believe you actually said that." She laughed, shaking her head. "Okay, Mr. Davis, lead on."

"First things first." He tilted her chin up and covered her mouth with his in a long, gentle kiss that left her trembling slightly. She leaned toward him, relishing the feel of his tongue flickering against hers. The moment he lifted his head, she missed him. Missed his feel and warmth and intoxicating aroma as he smiled down at her flushed face and stroked her cheek with his thumb.

"Oh, Kellen," she whispered.

"Let's . . . uh, . . ." He cleared his throat huskily. "Let's join Felicia and Timmy before I carry you out of here."

"Goodness, how very caveman of you."

"True, but I'm not kidding," he growled as he opened the door.

Paige could feel the warmth of Kellen's hand as he rested it on the small of her back. She forced a smile onto her lips, hoping it didn't appear too artificial as Kellen pushed the door inward. The irrational thought that she'd rather be going to the dentist popped into her mind as they stepped into the room.

"Kellen!" a feminine voice shouted, and in a blur of

flying red hair a woman rushed to him, throwing her arms around his neck and kissing him firmly on the mouth. Paige stepped back automatically as Kellen pulled the green-clad creature into his embrace and returned the kiss enthusiastically.

"Kellen, darling," the woman gushed when the kiss had finally been concluded, "it's divine to see you."

Divine? Divine! Paige frowned. Had she actually said *divine*? Lord.

"You look fantastic, Felicia," Kellen said.

"Thank you, love," Felicia said, kissing him quickly again. "And you are sexier than ever."

He grinned. "I try. Felicia, I'd like you to meet Paige Cunningham. Paige, Felicia Evans."

"I'm delighted, Paige," Felicia said with a warm smile. "Your dress is stunning. I wish I could wear something like that but with my red hair, I simply can't. And I'm too short for such a sophisticated design."

"I . . ."

"I always look like I'm going to the prom." Felicia frowned down at her green dress. "Oh, well, come eat. I am just starving and knowing Kellen, he is too. I certainly hope you like Mexican food, Paige. It occurred to me later that I was rather rude to decide for everyone where we would eat."

"It's one of my favorites." Paige smiled in spite of herself, warming to the gregarious actress.

"Nice to see you again, Paige," Timmy said.

"Hello, Timmy," Paige said.

"Sit by your lovely Paige, Kellen," Felicia said. "You and I will see enough of each other during the picture. My sweet Timmy is all mine tonight."

"I always do as I'm told," Kellen said with a grin, holding the back of the chair as Paige sat down.

"Ha!" Felicia said. "That's a joke. How can you

stand him, Paige? He's so spoiled and unbearably stubborn."

Paige laughed. "I know."

"I think you're in trouble, Kellen." Timmy chuckled. "These two ladies are definitely wise to you."

"This is an attractive room," Kellen said, causing the other three to burst into laughter.

When the waiter appeared to take their orders, Paige stole a closer look at Felicia Evans over the top of her menu. The star was beautiful, there was no denying it. Her copper-colored hair had a tousled appearance that had no doubt taken an hour to arrange. She was petite, and her features were small and perfect, as were her straight white teeth. A more than adequate bustline definitely erased the image of her going to a prom. Felicia Evans was a mature woman in every sense of the word, and had an unnerving way of gazing at a person through her long, sultry eyelashes. She was the female counterpart of Kellen's male sex-symbol image, and Paige suddenly felt like a Barbie doll that someone had dressed up and taken out to play. Yet Felicia had seemed friendly and had insisted that Kellen sit by Paige. Perhaps there were many sides to Felicia Evans, just as there were to Kellen. The tricky part, Paige told herself, was to know what was real and what wasn't.

As the drinks they had ordered were served, a stack of menus was set on the table and with a flourish the owner of the restaurant handed both Kellen and Felicia a pen. Paige watched as they concentrated on the task of autographing the large cardboard sheets until the job was completed. Beaming, the man collected his treasures and rushed from the room.

"Spare me, Felicia," Kellen said, raising his hand. "I've heard your sermonette on how ridiculous it is for people to get excited over someone's name scribbled on a piece of paper."

"Dumb, dumb, dumb," Felicia said, scowling slightly. "But I won't get started on that. Paige, I understand from Timmy that you're an interior decorator with the House of Martin."

"Yes, I am."

"Imagine putting together a whole house. I do good to make sure my shoes match my dress. I admire your talent, Paige."

"Well, thank you." Paige smiled. "But I must admit no one has ever asked for my autograph."

Felicia laughed. "Lucky you. I love your eyes. Can't you see those eyes on camera, Kellen? You should get Paige a screen test."

"No way," he said firmly. "I'm not sharing her with the whole world."

"Chauvinist!" Felicia said, leaning across the table and poking him in the chest. "Maybe she has an opinion on this, you know!"

"I don't care!" he said. "Paige isn't getting caught up in that mess and—"

"Children, please," Timmy said, raising his hands for silence. "Do behave yourselves. We have company, remember? Paige, if you see me aging before those gorgeous eyes in question you'll know why. Suffering through an entire filming with these two squabbling like three-year-olds will put me in an early grave."

"Sorry, Timmy," Felicia and Kellen said in unison as an uncontrollable giggle escaped from Paige's lips.

The food was delicious and the conversation lively. Paige found herself relaxing in the pleasant atmosphere. Kellen was extremely attentive, often reaching for her hand and smiling at her whenever their eyes met.

"Have you been studying your lines, Felicia?"

Timmy asked, after the waiter had removed the plates and poured the coffee.

"Yes, sir." She saluted and grinned. "I love the story. I swear though, Kellen, if you tickle me when we do those bed scenes, I'm going to break your nose!"

"Me?" he asked, his eyebrows raised in innocence. "I never laid a glove on you. You're the one who fell apart laughing without any help."

"Well, it was just so funny. Picture this, Paige. Kellen and I are supposed to be doing a hot-and-heavy number between the satin sheets, and he's whispering in my ear all the things he wants for lunch. I mean, how can I concentrate when this big ape is mumbling about hamburgers and fried chicken and pizza with pepperoni! I laughed so hard, I got the hiccups, and the shooting went into overtime that day."

"Kellen, you are terrible," Paige scolded him, trying not to sigh with relief. If all Kellen thought about was food when he was in bed with Felicia . . .

He shrugged. "I was hungry."

"As usual," Timmy chortled.

"Paige, sneak to the potty with me," Felicia said, pushing back her chair. "Just pray no one recognizes me."

Kellen and Timmy got to their feet as the two women rose and left the room. Kellen remained standing, staring at the door they closed behind them.

"Felicia looks great," Timmy said.

"Yes."

"She's very enthusiastic about the picture."

"Yes."

"Do you think it will snow?"

"Yes."

"All right, Kellen, come out of the ether and sit down," Timmy said.

"Huh?"

"Lord, man, Paige went to the ladies' room, not the moon! She'll be right back. What's wrong with you? Forget I asked. I already know."

"What's that supposed to mean?" Kellen scowled as he sank into the chair and stretched his long legs out in front of him.

"You've got it bad, boy." Timmy chuckled. "You watch over Paige as if you're afraid she's going to evaporate into thin air. Can't say as I blame you. She's a lovely woman. She brings out the protective instincts in a man because she seems so fragile, vulnerable. I must say though, I can't see her as being your type."

"Why not?" Kellen snapped angrily.

"Oh, I don't know," Timmy said, studying his fingernails. "You usually go for someone who understands the rules. The old have-a-good-time-while-it-lasts routine, and then call it a day. Paige is definitely not in that league."

"Of course not," Kellen said, hitting the table with the palm of his hand. "She's a real lady. Paige is special, Timmy. She's been through hell in the past, and she deserves to be happy."

"Can you do that, Kellen?" Timmy asked softly. "Can you make her happy?"

"I sure as hell can try."

"I see. Want my opinion?"

"No!"

"Tough, you're getting it. I think you're already in love with Paige Cunningham."

"Timmy, for Pete's sake," Kellen said, getting up and pacing the floor. "That's ridiculous."

"Is it? I've never seen you like this before. I'm betting that you're a goner."

"Dammit, Timmy."

"Okay. Okay. Forget I mentioned it. But if I were

you, I'd have a cozy chat with myself and find out how I feel about her."

"Yeah, right," Kellen mumbled, shoving his hands into his pockets.

"I wouldn't want to see you get hurt, Kellen," Timmy said quietly.

"Me?"

"Do you think you're immune to heartbreak because half the women in the country want you? Don't be so stupid. Kellen, you stepped out of the show-business glitter and into the real world when you found Paige. That means playing it straight and by a different game plan. You said yourself she's not the kind who would understand the hello–good-bye bit. We're talking commitment here. Words like *marriage* and *forever and ever* come to the front of my mind."

"Marriage!" Kellen roared. "Are you crazy?"

"I don't know." Timmy shrugged. "Am I?"

"I am not having this conversation."

"Whatever," Timmy said, a smile tugging at the corners of his mouth as Kellen resumed pacing in long, heavy strides.

"Lucked out," Felicia said as she fluffed her hair with her fingertips in front of the mirror in the powder room. "No one else is in here. Goodness, I'm stuffed, but that food was excellent."

"Yes, it was," Paige said.

"You know, Paige," Felicia said slowly, "I'm very close to Kellen. He's like family to me and, well, I just wanted to say I'm glad you're with him. I can't remember when he's looked so happy and relaxed. You've done that for him and I'm grateful. Kellen is an intense, complicated man. Of course, you realize by now that his lady-killer image is a bunch of bull. I mean, he's gorgeous but he certainly doesn't go around stomping on hearts for the fun of it. That's all for publicity. But the way that man looks at you—I swear, he keeps forgetting Timmy and I are in the room. Are you in love with Kellen?"

"What?" Paige gasped, her eyes wide in shock.

"Don't faint on me here. It's a reasonable question."

"It certainly is not," Paige snapped. "Me? In love with Kellen Davis? Really, Felicia, that's absurd."

"Why?"

"Because . . . because I hardly know him!"

"So?"

"I mean, well, I feel as though I've known him for a long time, but in actuality I— Granted, he's very handsome and extremely thoughtful, and when he laughs, his eyes look like sapphires and, uh . . . I think we'd better get back." Paige quickly left the room.

"Oh, boy. Oh, boy." Felicia laughed. "I wouldn't miss this for the world. And I'm going to have a front-row seat the whole time I'm in town."

Kellen glanced up anxiously when Paige reentered the room with a smiling Felicia. He met Paige's gaze in a long, studying look. They were each held riveted in place as if they were seeing the other for the first time.

Felicia cleared her throat noisily and winked at Timmy. He swallowed a chuckle and got to his feet. "I promised you an early evening, Felicia," he said. "You have a long day tomorrow."

"You're right, darling, and I have jet lag to boot. Off we go. Kellen, I'll see you bright and early. Kellen?"

"Huh? Oh, right, Felicia. Great being with you this evening. We'll have a ball doing this picture," Kellen said.

"Paige," Felicia said, hugging her quickly, "the first free day I get, we'll have lunch, okay?"

Paige smiled. "Yes, I'd like that."

"So long for now." Felicia waved, linked arms with Timmy, and literally dragged the older man out of the room.

Paige avoided Kellen's piercing eyes and sank into a chair, her trembling legs suddenly unable to support her. Felicia was wrong, she told herself firmly. There was nothing unusual about Kellen's behavior toward her. And as for her being in love with him, Felicia had simply been watching too many of her own movies! Paige knew exactly what she was doing in this relationship with Kellen. She wouldn't even see Kellen after tonight. He—

"Paige? Are you all right?"

"Yes. Yes, of course. I think perhaps I should be getting home."

Nodding, Kellen helped her on with her coat, and in a few minutes they were driving toward her apartment.

"Did you have a nice time?" Kellen asked, breaking the silence that had enveloped them for several miles.

"Yes, I did. You were right. Felicia is a very warm, down-to-earth person. I sincerely liked her."

"Good," Kellen said absently as Timmy's words continued to ramble through his mind. Dammit, he was not in love with Paige! He refused to be. Okay, so she was different from anyone he'd ever known, and he found her unique and beautiful and incredibly honest, but in love with her? No way! Timmy was cracking up. Marriage? Next he'd have him bouncing babies on his knee and going to P.T.A. meetings. He realized that Paige didn't enter into relationships lightly, but he'd made no promises. He'd done nothing to hurt her. But he'd never experienced anything like this with anyone else. She *should* be a mother.

Think of what a baby girl would look like with Paige's great big eyes and—

"Kellen, you missed my street."

"Damn it to hell," he roared, smacking his hand against the steering wheel.

"Don't throw a tantrum! Just drive around the block."

"Sorry," he growled.

A strange tension seemed to move in and shroud them in a stiff silence as Kellen escorted Paige into the elevator and along the corridor to her door. She handed him her key without looking at him and switched on the light as they entered the living room.

"I'll take care of the remaining work on the decorating," she said, turning to face him.

"Fine."

"You'll be given a detailed accounting of all the expenses. I hope it will meet with your approval. I know you'll be too busy to offer your opinions on what I select."

"I trust your judgment."

"Yes, well, I— Kellen, these days we've spent together have been wonderful. I'm very glad you touched my life."

"Paige, I—"

"I'm really quite tired, so I'll say good night," she said quickly, acutely aware she was fighting back unexpected tears. "I wish you success on your picture."

"What are you trying to get across here?" he said fiercely. "If this is a brush-off, you're not being too subtle."

"I'm being realistic, Kellen. We snatched a few hours together, and now it's over. You're going back to your world and I'm returning to mine."

"Just like that?" he roared angrily. "Is that all this has meant to you?"

"No! What we shared was— I'll treasure the memories, Kellen. You made me laugh again, feel alive and whole. I'm grateful for—"

"Grateful! What an insane word! You make it sound as if I did you a favor. Dammit, Paige, we gave and took equally. I've never felt so— You are not dusting me off, lady. This is not the end, because it's just the beginning!"

"Of what? Oh, Kellen, wake up." Paige wrapped her arms tightly around herself as a shiver swept through her. "If we walk away now, we can still smile. Don't push this thing. We have no future together, and prolonging the good-bye will only cause pain. I'm so tired of crying, Kellen. Leave me with what I have."

"And what about me? Don't I have a voice in this decision?"

"You'll move on to make your next picture and—"

"And what?" he said, coming to her and cupping her face in his hands. "Forget those chocolate-chip eyes of yours? Forget the feel of your soft skin and the aroma of your perfume? Forget this . . .?"

With a searing, hungry kiss Kellen claimed her mouth, his tongue meeting hers in an almost angry assault. Paige pushed against his chest as a sudden wave of panic swept over her. Her attempts to struggle out of his tightening grasp were futile, and she felt the familiar stirrings of desire begin deep within her. She relaxed in his arms, leaning against the hard contours of his body. Kellen's kiss became gentle, warm, sensuous as he stroked the soft material covering her slender hips. His lips placed fluttering kisses over her eyes, cheeks, down the column of her neck to the tops of her pulsating breasts.

"No, Paige," he said huskily, "I won't let you go. Not now. Not yet. We'll have Christmas together. Agree to that much. Please, Paige."

"I—"

"Christmas, Paige," he whispered, his hands caressing her breasts and sending shock waves throughout all of her trembling body.

"Yes, yes, we'll . . . share Christmas," she said, her voice hushed and shaky.

"I want you. God, how I want you, Paige."

And she wanted him. Oh, yes, she thought, she wanted Kellen with every fiber of her being, every breath in her body. "I want you, Kellen. You make me so glad I'm a woman."

"Oh, Paige," he moaned, kissing her again and then lifting her into his arms and carrying her into the bedroom.

What had she done? Paige thought as Kellen laid her gently on the bed. It was supposed to have been over tonight. Finished. But now she'd agreed to share Christmas with Kellen. She wouldn't be alone and miserable this year. She'd think about the rest tomorrow. Now she wanted Kellen to make love to her, hold her, caress her. "Come to me, Kellen," she whispered, lifting her arms to receive him as he covered her body with his.

"Your pretty dress. I'm wrinkling it."

"Then maybe I should take it off," she said boldly, reaching up to unbutton his shirt.

She heard his sharp intake of breath as she slid her hand inside the silky material and over the corded muscles of his chest. He moved off of her to rid himself of his restricting clothing and watched as Paige rose from the bed and stepped out of her dress and slip. He grasped her hand to stop her as she reached to unclasp her bra. He himself slowly removed the wispy material and then caressed her breasts, first with his passion-filled sapphire blue eyes, then with the gentle stroking of his thumbs. His lips moved to where his maddening touch had been, drawing first one rosy nipple into his mouth and then the other.

Paige moaned softly as Kellen's pleasure-giving journey continued over her trembling body to her flat stomach and beyond as he drew her panties down her slender legs. He stood again to pull her close, pressing her hips against his. She felt his arousal announcing his need and relished the knowledge that his desire for her was equal to the aching fire that swirled within her.

Again he scooped her into his arms, holding her tightly as he covered her mouth in a demanding kiss. He placed her on the bed and stretched out next to her, his tongue tracing the outline of her breast until he finally drew the taut bud into his mouth. Heat surged through her body as he moved to the other ivory mound. She ran her hands down his back, relishing the feel of the strong muscles beneath her fingers. Never before had she been filled with such a burning fire of passion and desire. She ached for him to consume her totally. She pressed her hips closer to his body, feeling his arousal, seeking the ultimate goal. He was magnificent, Paige thought. Every inch of him was a bold declaration of his masculinity. His skin was evenly tanned, his body proportioned so perfectly, it was as though he had been sculpted by the finest artist in the land.

Kellen hesitated, only to have Paige circle his neck with her arms, arching her back to bring him closer, to fill her being with his manhood. His rhythmic motions started in a slow, beating pulse, building to a crescendo of ecstasy that was matched perfectly by her willing body. Higher they went in unison, like a finely tuned symphony that produced a celebration of bursting colors and roaring senses. Their bodies glistened as they drifted back, Kellen resting on his elbows as he gazed at Paige's flushed face.

"Heavenly," he whispered.

"Oh, yes," she said, stroking his rugged cheek with her fingertips.

"Paige, I— I—"

"What is it, Kellen?"

"It's late," he said, moving off her and then pulling her close. "I have to be on location early. Maybe I should go so I don't disturb you when I get up."

"You try to leave this bed, mister, I'll break your toe."

"No! That's awful." He chuckled. "How could I be sexy in front of the cameras with a broken toe?"

"Good point. You'd better stay. Think of your public."

"I'd rather think about waking up next to you in the morning, Paige."

"Hold that thought," she said, trying to stifle a yawn.

"Good night, Paige Cunningham," he said, kissing her on the forehead after pulling the blankets over them.

"Sweet dreams, Kellen Davis," she murmured as she closed her eyes.

He had bought himself a little time, Kellen thought, staring into the darkness. She had really been going to end it tonight! Okay, so he was safe through the holidays. Lord, listen to him! He sounded like a kid who was frantic that the head cheerleader wouldn't like him anymore. What was it about this woman that sent him into a tailspin? Never mind, he'd figure it out later. Tonight Paige was in his arms, and that was good enough for him. Good? Hell, it was terrific.

She had come to him in total abandonment, had given of herself so willingly, trustingly. He had never experienced such passion. It hadn't been just sex. They had made love, and for the first time in his life he understood the difference. He didn't know what was happening to him, but one thing was certain. He had found Paige and he didn't want to let her go!

Kellen allowed fatigue to claim him and drifted off to sleep, his head resting on the pillow beside Paige's. Their bodies were entwined in comfortable possessiveness through the remaining hours of the night.

Soft, nibbling kisses on her face brought Paige from a deep, dreamless sleep, and she opened her eyes and blinked in the darkness.

"I didn't want you to wake up and find I'd gone," Kellen whispered. "Go right back to sleep."

"What time is it?"

"Four thirty."

"Ugh."

"I'll call you tonight but I don't know when. The first day of shooting is a killer."

"I'll get up and make you some breakfast, Kellen."

"No, stay put. I have to go to my house and change. I'll grab something there. Have a good day, pretty Paige. Thank you for a wonderful night."

"I wish—"

"Me too. Close your beautiful brown eyes."

"But—"

"Shhh." He silenced her with a long kiss that sent sparklers of desire dancing through her body. "Bye for now."

"Good-bye, Kellen."

Paige listened intently until she heard the front door being closed quietly, then snuggled down under the blankets. As she drifted back into a peaceful slumber she hugged the pillow that held the male aroma of Kellen Davis.

At nine o'clock sharp Paige entered the House of Martin and startled Janet, who had her nose pushed into the morning paper.

"Oh, Mrs. Cunningham, I— Oh, I—"

"Calm down," Paige said. "I didn't mean to scare

you to death. I never knew the newspaper could be so enthralling."

"I— This piece in the society section says that— Oh, please, Mrs. Cunningham, tell me what he's really like. Are his eyes really that blue? What did he wear? Did he—"

"What are you talking about?" Paige interrupted, frowning.

"Here, look. It says, 'Kellen Davis was seen once again last night in the company of our city's own Paige Cunningham, a talented interior decorator for the House of Martin. After an evening of dining and dancing at the Majestic, the couple once again stepped out on the town, this time in the company of Felicia Evans and Timmy Winslow. It would seem that Ms. Cunningham has taken first seat with the handsome Mr. Davis, pushing Miss Evans out of the limelight. It will be interesting to observe if angry sparks fly on the set today when the actor and actress meet. As for Paige Cunningham, it was apparent to this reporter that she has more on her mind than matching sofas with chairs. Felicia Evans had best be on her toes.' "

"My God," Paige whispered, grabbing the paper and scanning the article as the color drained from her face.

"Did you have an absolutely awesome time with Kellen Davis?" Janet asked breathlessly.

"Paige," Paul said suddenly.

"What? Oh, good morning, Paul," Paige said, her eyes still riveted to the paper.

"May I see you in my office?"

"Yes, of course," she said absently.

"Now!"

Frowning at the sharp tone of Paul's voice, Paige dropped the newspaper onto Janet's desk and followed Paul down the hall and into his office. He sat down behind his desk and scowled at her as she took the chair opposite.

"I want to know what in the hell is going on between you and Davis," he said angrily.

"What do you mean?" she snapped.

"Janet could hardly wait to show me the juicy tidbit in the paper. Now I know why I haven't heard from you. You've been too busy being bowled over by Mr. Body Beautiful!"

"Now, wait just a minute, Paul," she retorted, getting to her feet. "You have no right to—"

"Interfere in your personal life? No, I suppose not. But, dammit, they linked you with the House of Martin, and that affects me and my reputation here. I've had calls this morning from two of our dowager queens, asking if it's true that you're involved with the racy Kellen Davis. It seems you've promised them color swatches or whatever, and they're worried that your time will be taken up with your glorious love affair."

"You can tell those rich bitches I'll deliver on schedule," Paige said, trying desperately to hang on to her temper. "Is that all, Mr. Martin?"

"No, it is not! Sit down!"

"No!"

"Oh, man," Paul said quietly, massaging the back of his neck. "Paige, you know I don't care what those old ladies think. I'm worried about you."

"Paul, please don't be," she said, sinking back into the chair. "I can—"

"Yeah, I know, take care of yourself. But, sweetheart, you're wrong. You're out of your league with Davis. He'll hurt you, Paige, I swear it. Haven't you had enough pain in your life?"

"You don't even know Kellen. He's a very warm, caring—"

"He's really got you snowed, doesn't he? The man is

an actor! He knows exactly what performance will get him where he wants to go. He's a phoney!"

"No!"

"Stop seeing him, Paige," Paul said, his voice cold and flat.

"Don't tell me what to do, Paul," she said, her brown eyes flashing with anger. "Now, if you'll excuse me, I have to line up the painters to do Kellen's living room."

"Paige, listen to me! You're making a terrible mistake. Davis is—"

"I'll keep you fully up-to-date on my progress on the Kellen Davis decorating commission, Mr. Martin," she said stiffly as she walked to the door. "Beyond that, kindly stay out of my life!" She managed not to slam the door as she left the office.

Paige was trembling so badly, she barely made it down the corridor and into her office, where she sank into the leather chair behind her desk. Covering her face with her hands, she shook her head to try to erase the terrible scene with Paul from her tormented thoughts. They had never exchanged a cross word before. Never. He was livid about the article in the newspaper, but then so was she! They had no right to print those things, she thought fiercely. How dare they infringe on her privacy, make her sound like just another one of Kellen Davis's many women. It sounded sordid, ugly, as if Kellen was flaunting her in front of Felicia. Damn those reporters. What she and Kellen had together didn't belong to the world. It was theirs! And now Paul was furious. Oh, hell's bells, what a mess!

Forcing herself to push aside the anguish in her mind, Paige picked up the telephone and dialed the number of the painter she used most frequently. Scott Howlett worked efficiently and produced flawless work for Paige's picky clientele.

"Howlett's," a deep voice answered on the second ring.

"Scott? Paige Cunningham. Save my life and say you can do a wallpaper stripping and repainting number for me super fast."

"Let me guess. It's for Kellen Davis."

"How did . . ."

"My wife reads the society column. You met her at that party last year, remember? She's all thrilled to think she knows you because you're seeing Kellen Davis. It's her new claim to fame."

"Oh, no," Paige moaned.

"Hey, I think it's great, Paige. You and Kellen Davis must look terrific together. About time you put a little spice in your life."

"Scott, can you do the job or not?" Paige said sharply.

"Sure. I'm no fool. My wife would shoot me if I turned down the chance to see the inside of Kellen Davis's house. I'll have to memorize every corner so I can tell her what it was like. I'll be a hero."

"Can you meet me there at one to do an estimate?"

"Yep. Give me the address. How much are we stripping?"

"Just the living room for now."

"Oh, really?" Scott laughed. "From what I've read about Kellen Davis, I thought it would be his bedroom. No offense meant, of course, Paige."

"Good-bye, Scott," Paige said coolly. "I'll see you at one."

"Hey! The address!"

Paige rattled off the directions to Kellen's house and then slammed the receiver into place. Did the whole city of Phoenix read the morning paper? she thought angrily. She felt as though she were in a fishbowl with thousands of eyes staring at her. She hated this! She was going to go buy Kellen some furniture and forget this madness.

Out in the corridor Paige glanced down to Paul's office, only to see that the door was closed. With a deep sigh of regret over the heated words they had exchanged, she walked out of the House of Martin into the crisp air of the sunny day.

By noon Paige's nerves were so jangled, she could hardly consume the soup and salad she had ordered at a small café. She had successfully put together another grouping for Kellen's enormous living room, but the morning had been a nightmare. Every store where she had stopped to inspect their selections was a place she was well-known, and to her dismay the Phoenix morning paper had done a booming business that day. She had smiled her way through endless questions regarding her relationship with the marvelous Kellen Davis, changing the subject as quickly as possible. One of the men had winked at her as if to indicate he knew what she was doing with the sex symbol, and a woman in another store had simply gawked at Paige as if she were the eighth wonder of the world.

"Ridiculous," Paige mumbled into her coffee cup. "People are weird. I've been stared at so much this morning, I feel as though I forgot to put my clothes on. I definitely, absolutely hate this."

"Pardon me?" the waitress said, stopping at the table.

"Oh, nothing. May I have my bill, please?"

"Certainly."

The stormy expression on Paige's face made it perfectly clear to Scott Howlett that she was meeting him to discuss business and nothing else. He quickly surveyed the living room, quoted a price that Paige accepted, and agreed to meet her there with his crew at nine the next morning. She spent the afternoon scouring small shops for unusual knickknacks to add to Kellen's bookshelves. The trunk and backseat of her car were loaded with the treasures as dusk fell over the desert and she headed for home. In a rush of panic she remembered she had not checked in with Paul and stopped at a telephone booth to make the call.

"The House of Martin."

"Janet? Mrs. Cunningham. Please tell Mr. Martin I've been in the field all day and will be again tomorrow."

"Do I have to?"

"What?"

"He's been a grouch all day. I've never known him to be so crabby. I think I'll slide the note under his door."

"He's just a little upset about something, Janet."

"Yeah, I know. He's having a fit because of you and Kellen Davis. I heard him yelling at you this morning. But, jeez, Mrs. Cunningham, who could resist Kellen Davis? I think it's neat that you're having an . . . I mean, that you two are, uh—"

"Good night, Janet," Paige said wearily, and hung up the receiver.

Paige's head was throbbing and her feet hurt by the time she had made two extra trips to her car to unload her purchases from the backseat. She was afraid to leave the valuable merchandise in plain view overnight, but was already dreading repeating the performance the next morning to take the stuff to Kellen's home.

She switched on the television to catch the news and kicked off her shoes before sinking onto the sofa with an exhausted sigh. Suddenly she sat up straight as the announcer's words reached her and the picture focused.

". . . here in Phoenix to produce his new picture,

Love Me Less," the woman reporter was saying as she smiled into the camera. "Mr. Davis has already been rumored to be seeing our own lovely Paige Cunningham of the exclusive House of Martin decorating firm. I asked Mr. Davis about his supposedly torrid romance with Felicia Evans and how he could possibly juggle both of these beautiful women with his already busy schedule."

"You witch," Paige yelled.

Suddenly Kellen's handsome, smiling face filled the screen. His hair was tousled by the wind, and his blue shirt had several buttons undone, revealing more than a glimpse of his massive tanned chest. Paige felt a tingle run through her at the sight of him, but ignored the sensations, leaning forward to hear how he would reply to the probing, suggestive question.

"Tell her, Kellen," Paige whispered, clutching her hands together. "Explain that there's nothing going on between you and Felicia. Make that reporter understand that what you and I have together is no one's business. Please, Kellen, stop this nightmare before it goes any further!"

Six

Paige's eyes widened in horror, and she was hardly breathing as she heard Kellen answer the reporter in a deep, sexy voice.

"Felicia and I . . . have an understanding," he said, flashing a dazzling smile. "As for Paige Cunningham, well, she's decorating the home I recently purchased here."

"Do you intend on continuing to see Ms. Cunningham?"

"It's a big house." He grinned and shrugged.

"I see." The woman smiled, nodded, and all but giggled.

The camera switched back to the announcer, who quickly wiped the smile from her face, cleared her throat, and said, "In other news today . . ."

A sob escaped from Paige's lips as she stumbled to the television and turned it off. She dropped to her knees as tears spilled over onto her cheeks. She had no idea how long she had been crying when she finally dragged herself to her feet and walked numbly into the kitchen to fix herself a cup of tea. Sitting down at the table, she stared into the steaming liquid, her mind whirling with anguished thoughts.

Kellen's words seemed to strike at her with an unrelenting force. His veiled innuendos had been degrading as he more than implied that he was continuing his affair with Felicia Evans and, since the opportunity had presented itself, would carry on with Paige as well. Even his smile had been provocative, his body language sensuous as he spoke of the two women he had been romantically linked with by the media.

The hurt and pain of Kellen's betrayal slowly dissipated as Paige's emotions changed into a cold anger that settled over her. Kellen had allowed, even assisted, in shooting her reputation straight to hell! He knew, dammit, he knew what they had shared was special, wonderful, rare. But in spite of that he had put the importance of maintaining his sex-symbol reputation first, above everything else, including her. That louse! How dare he take the precious moments from their private world and use them to further his own image for the public! Kellen understood, as she did, that they weren't playing a game, weren't simply indulging in a casual sexual fling. But the bum had sure made it sound like that was exactly what it was for his adoring fans. Well, no more, Paige vowed. She had seen Kellen Davis for the last time!

Give Mr. Davis another Oscar for an outstanding performance, she thought bitterly. Dear heaven, he was despicable!

The ringing of the telephone startled her out of her angry, tangled thoughts, and she rose instinctively to answer it. Her hand froze in midair just above the receiver as the image of Kellen's handsome face flashed before her eyes. Her throat felt tight and dry as she stared at the screaming instrument. Unconsciously she backed away, covering her ears against the shrill sound that only added to the turbulence in her mind. At last the ringing stopped, and in blessed silence she walked into the bathroom, where she undressed and stepped into a steaming shower.

She allowed the water to beat against her body as she fought desperately to regain control of her shattered emotions. Why had Kellen done it? How could his damnable reputation mean more to him than she did?

The questions remained unanswered as Paige crept beneath the blankets on the bed and stared into the darkness. The stillness of the room seemed to press upon her like an unbearable weight. The happiness, the newfound joy she had discovered with Kellen, was destroyed. She had agreed to spend Christmas with him—and now? She had nothing but the haunting ghosts of the past to keep her company.

A strange calmness settled over her as a horrible thought struck her to the inner core. It was not the memories of Jerry that would plague her through the holidays. Jerry Cunningham was gone forever. The ache in her heart was new. It was a yearning for the touch and sight and sound of Kellen Davis, and Paige knew she would never be the same again.

Bittersweet, she thought suddenly. So many moments of ecstasy to hold so tightly in her heart. Lovemaking that was incredibly beautiful, exquisite. She had started out using Kellen as a crutch to get her through this season but then . . . Oh, no, how had it happened? At what point in those stolen hours had she fallen in love with him? And, God help her, she did love him. She did!

"Well, hell!" she said angrily, sitting up in the bed. Now she had really gone and done it! She had fallen in love with Kellen Davis and had no one to blame but herself. But she was not going to wallow in self-pity this time! She refused. Kellen was rotten. A publicity-grabbing con man, but for a while he had been hers and they'd shared precious times. She'd have her Christmas and make it just fine on her own. Why was she in that bed? She was hungry!

With a new, firm resolve Paige padded barefoot into the kitchen and fixed a dinner of bacon and eggs. She was drinking one more cup of coffee when the telephone rang again. She sat perfectly still, willing herself not to move. With a satisfied nod she waited until the ringing stopped and then busied herself cleaning up after her meal. A wave of fatigue settled over her, and she returned to the warmth of the bed, pulling the blankets up to her chin. A single tear slid down her cheek, and she brushed it away in angry frustration at her own weakness before flopping over onto her stomach and falling into a restless sleep.

When the alarm went off, announcing shrilly in no uncertain terms that the new day had begun, Paige shut it off roughly. With a moan she burrowed her head into her pillow. She had dreamed of Kellen through the endless night, seeing his face, hearing his laughter. There would be no way to stop the dreams and she knew that. She would simply have to learn to live with the pictures that would dance before her eyes as even her subconscious called out to be with him during the dark lonely hours.

Walking into the bathroom, she glanced at her reflection in the mirror. Her large dark eyes stared back at her. The haunted look that had been so familiar since Jerry's death was gone, but there was no sparkle, no excitement—simply a quiet dullness that registered nothing.

She was in love, she thought ruefully. Her eyes should be glowing at the very thought of Kellen. But it would take his returned love to make that happen, and that would never be. If only they could have had a little more time. If only they had parted in gentleness and caring, leaving the memories untarnished by the words he had spoken in that interview. If only . . .

Wrapping her arms around herself, she remembered the feel of his hands caressing her. Holding herself tightly, she clung to the desire that surged within her as she pictured his taut, muscular body moving over her. She could almost smell his after-shave and the fresh aroma of soap that lingered long after he had left her. Her breasts throbbed as she recalled the tantalizing touch of his fingertips and lips over the sensitive mounds. Oh, how she wanted him. Needed him. Loved him. Her mind seemed to be filled with the sound of the beating of her racing heart, and again unwanted tears spilled onto her pale cheeks. Taking a shaking breath, she forced herself to smile, practicing looking cheerful and carefree as she thrust aside the heavy ache in her heart.

Dressed in navy-blue slacks and blazer with a pale blue silk blouse tied in a soft bow at her neck, she pulled her thick dark hair back into a tight bun at the nape of her neck. She appeared calm, cool, and professional and, tilting her nose slightly in the air, she marched into the living room.

"Wonderful," she muttered, seeing the forgotten boxes she had toted up the stairs the evening before. An hour later she was driving toward Kellen's house to keep her appointment with Scott Howlett.

Nothing like jumping right into the fire, she thought, a frown creasing her brow. Kellen's home was filled with memories of him and what they had shared together. Perhaps this was best. She'd have no opportunity to run. She'd walk right in there, do her job to the best of her ability, and somehow, somehow survive.

Scott and his crew were waiting for her when she pulled up in front of the house, and he waved cheerfully as she got out of the car. He quickly ordered his men to carry in the numerous boxes for Paige and then whistled low and long as they entered the house.

"This is some place," he said. "Who's moving in? The Fifth Army?"

"Cozy, huh?" Paige laughed. "Well, you do your thing on that awful wallpaper, and I'll tackle finishing the bookshelves."

"Say, Paige," Scott said, "you don't suppose Davis will show up, do you? My wife would sure be excited if I could tell her I'd actually met the great man."

"I doubt it," she said. "He's started the production of the film."

"Oh." Scott grinned at her. "I thought he'd make a special point of being here to see his . . . decorator."

A flash of anger swept through Paige, and it was a moment before she could compose herself enough to speak. "Are you by any chance referring to the interview Kellen gave on television last night, Scott?" she asked, her voice low and tight.

"Hey, I didn't mean to upset you or anything," he said quickly. "I just figured you were having a good old time with Davis. He sure made it sound like—"

"I *know* how it sounded," she snapped. "Mr. Davis has a real flair with words. I would suggest to you, Scott, that if you want to live to see lunchtime, you'll change the subject."

"Got it." He nodded. "My mouth is glued shut. Okay, you guys, let's get to work. The boss lady here is on the warpath."

Damn you, Kellen Davis, Paige fumed. She'd like to punch him right in his gorgeous nose!

After tossing Scott one more stormy glare, Paige began the task of arranging the bookshelves next to the fireplace. The ashes in the hearth were cold and dark and held no resemblance to the warm fire she had sat in front of with Kellen. It seemed like an eternity since she had been held in his strong but gentle arms, tasted the sweetness of his kiss. He had entered her life and then left it in such a short expanse of time that many would probably feel it wasn't worth mentioning. But Kellen Davis had come, he had seen her, and oh, Lord, how he had conquered.

Borrowing a ladder from Scott, Paige climbed to the top to continue her chore. By distributing the books and knickknacks in clever arrangements, she would give the shelves the appearance of being completed when in actuality they could hold a great deal more. The morning flew by, and Paige looked up in surprise when Scott asked if she wanted one of the sandwiches his wife had packed for his lunch.

"I'd love it," she said, coming down off the ladder. "Not that I deserve it, the way I bit your head off."

"Forget it," Scott said, sitting next to her on the floor. "I apparently was way out of line. After that stuff in the paper and then Davis's bit on television, I thought—"

"I know," Paige said quietly, unwrapping the sandwich. "Let's drop it, okay?"

"Sure."

The two discussed the plans for the color scheme for the living room and shared a thermos of coffee. The other workmen had chosen to eat outside on the front porch in the sunshine, and one opened the front door and announced the arrival of a delivery truck.

"Right on time," Paige said, getting to her feet. "I'll have them bring the furniture on in and then we'll cover it with drop cloths."

"Is everything for this room coming today?" Scott asked.

"No. I wasn't that lucky because of the Christmas rush. It's strung out over the next two days."

"Good. Less for me to stumble over. Nothing worse than a klutzy painter."

Again painful memories assaulted Paige as each piece of furniture was brought into the room. She vividly recalled the time of day, the conversation she had had with Kellen over the selection, his stubborn refusal to give in on something he wanted once he had made up his mind. They had spent such marvelous hours selecting the items for his home, and he had spoken often of their sitting together on the enormous sofa in front of the fire.

One thing was for certain, she thought, sighing deeply: There would be someone else next to him. Kellen wouldn't be alone for very long.

"Scott," she said quickly, refusing to dwell on her gloomy thoughts, "I'm going into town to do some more shopping for this place. I'll be back by five to lock up."

"Okay." He waved absently.

The afternoon proved tiring but productive. Paige found a butcher-block table and eight wooden chairs to replace the rickety set now in Kellen's kitchen. She arrived back at the large house just as Scott was loading the last of his supplies into his truck. She agreed to meet him there at nine the next morning and then walked across the wide front porch to lock the door. The sound of an approaching car reached her ears, and she spun around in alarm, registering a wave of relief that it was Timmy Winslow behind the wheel and not Kellen.

"Hello," she called as he stepped out of the vehicle.

"Greetings, my dear," he said, joining her on the porch.

"I was just about to lock up, Timmy. I'm afraid things are a bit of a mess in there."

"That's understandable. Do join me for a cup of coffee before you go, Paige."

"Well, I—"

"Please. It's been a grueling day and I could use the company of someone from the sane world."

"All right," Paige said, "but I can only stay a minute." She couldn't run the risk of seeing Kellen. She wasn't that tough yet. She was liable to fall apart and she'd hate herself if she did.

"Why are you here, Timmy?" Paige asked, following him into the kitchen. "A house being painted is the worst place in the world to be."

"I thoroughly agree with you. I've come on the extremely important mission of checking the cupboards and refrigerator to see what Kellen needs in the way of groceries. I am often issued these high-class assignments, you understand." Timmy laughed as he set two mugs of water in the microwave oven. "We're roughing it with instant coffee. I do apologize."

"Instant is certainly acceptable," Paige said, sitting down gingerly on the wobbly picnic bench. "By the way, as of tomorrow, there will be a real live dining-room set in here."

"Oh? Too bad. I was getting attached to this one. It's so unique."

"That's not quite the word I would have used," Paige said with a laugh, accepting her drink from Timmy as he sat down opposite her.

"So, tell me, Paige," Timmy said, "what did you think of Felicia?"

"I liked her. I wasn't sure what to expect, but I found her very pleasant."

"And Kellen?" he asked, looking at her over the rim of his cup.

"Pardon me?"

"What have you discovered about Kellen Davis?" Timmy said quietly.

"I thought I knew him, Timmy, but I've since discovered I was mistaken. Listen, I really must be going."

"Paige, you're upset about what Kellen said during the television interview, aren't you?"

"Timmy, please." Paige got up from the table. "I really don't want to discuss this. There's no point in hashing over what has already been done. I made a terrible error in judgment, and I have no one to blame but myself. I just want to forget it."

"Can you do that?" Timmy asked gently. "Are you capable of erasing Kellen from your mind?"

"Of course," she snapped. "Now I really must go."

"I told him he had really made a mistake when he talked to that reporter, but he assured me that you understood that it was necessary that he maintain his image."

"What?" she shrieked. "He honestly feels he had the right to destroy my reputation so he'd appear sexier for his damnable female following? Well, I've got news for Mr. Davis! He can take a long walk off a short pier. Good night, Timmy." She turned and marched from the room.

"I knew it. I knew it," Timmy muttered, shaking his head. "Kellen, my boy, you're in hot water."

Paige was trembling with anger as she drove back into town in the gathering dusk. The sky had been transformed into a fairyland of color. The clouds, in hues of purple and yellow, were stacked in layers like fluffy mounds of whipped cream as they wove their way across the face of the mountains. Paige took no notice of nature's artistry as she put miles between herself and Kellen's house.

Unbelievable, she thought. Kellen Davis was incredible! He actually believed she'd go along with his degrading statement about her without blinking an eye? How she despised that man!

Sighing deeply, Paige immediately sensed the untruth of her own statement. How much easier it all would be if she could hate Kellen, but that was impossible. She loved him, and that fact was rapidly making her life terribly complicated. She was forced to spend hours in his home, which was overflowing with memories of the time they had spent together. She was creating a lovely atmosphere in which Kellen could charm the next woman who struck his fancy. How dare that man use her to further his machismo appeal! In love with Kellen Davis or not, she would thoroughly enjoy giving the big lug a piece of her mind!

Paige's muscles were complaining from the endless trips up and down the ladder, and her first order of business, she decided, would be a long, leisurely soak in the bathtub. Her steps were slow and heavy as she left the elevator and headed for her apartment, but she gasped in surprise when she saw who was waiting for her.

"Paul!" she said, hurrying toward him. "I didn't expect to—"

"I want to talk to you," he said, his face set in an angry frown. "Now."

He had seen the television interview, she thought bleakly as she inserted her key in the lock and preceded Paul into the apartment. He turned immediately to face her, his grim expression leaving no doubt as to his frame of mind.

"You have really done it this time," he bellowed, his

fury erupting at full volume. "You and your lover dragged the House of Martin's reputation through the mud on the six o'clock news, for heaven's sake!"

"Paul—"

"Dammit, Paige, I can't believe you'd do this to me. My phone hasn't stopped ringing all day. My top decorator is playing beddy-bye with a sex symbol, and I'm coming out looking like a fool. There have even been crank calls asking when the swinging Ms. Cunningham would be free to redo half the bedrooms in Phoenix. Two of your clients want someone else assigned to them since they've decided you're much too involved in your damnable affair to give them proper attention!"

"Oh, my God," Paige whispered, sinking onto a chair. "I never dreamed that—"

"That what?" Paul roared. "You could sleep with someone like Davis and keep it away from the media? Are you really that naive? They never mention your name without connecting you to the House of Martin. I saw Davis smirking on television, making it perfectly clear that his decorator was providing much more than just a nicely arranged living room!"

"I had no idea he was going to do that," Paige yelled, jumping to her feet and planting her hands on her hips. "You're behaving as though I condone his lovely little speech. I would never have done anything to hurt your reputation or mine, Paul."

"You should have thought of that before you went to bed with him!"

"Paul Martin, you have no right to stand there and pass judgment on my personal life!"

"I sure as hell do when your actions involve my firm and the prestige and respect I've worked long and hard to establish in this city. I'm no saint, Paige, but I'm at least discreet in my affairs, and I've never landed smack-dab in the middle of a news broadcast!"

"It wasn't my fault!" Paige screamed, knowing that wasn't the most mature statement she had ever made, but refraining at least from stamping her foot.

"Oh, right," Paul said sarcastically. "Davis clubbed you over the head and dragged you into his den of iniquity. You knew exactly what you were doing, with absolutely no regard for what it might do to the House of Martin."

"Paul! That's not fair!"

"I've been urging you to start living again, Paige, but you didn't have to go crazy!"

"I—" Paige started, then turned in surprise as a knock sounded at the door. She ignored the summons, only to let out an exasperated sigh when it was repeated. She flung the door open. Her eyes widened in shock as Kellen's massive frame loomed before her. "Kellen," she gasped.

"Paige." He nodded, no smile on his handsome face as he moved past her into the room. He stopped immediately when he saw Paul, and the two men glared at each other.

This is not happening, Paige thought wildly. It was insane! Did she introduce them and serve tea and crumpets? Oh, help!

"I need to speak to you, Paige," Kellen said, his eyes still riveted on Paul. "Alone."

"Don't let me stop you," Paul snarled. "I'm only one man. The whole city knows your business."

"Paul, don't, please," Paige said, wringing her hands nervously.

"Ah, so this is Paul Martin," Kellen said, his voice sounding calm, but the twitching muscle in his jaw very evident.

"Of the House of Martin," Paul said. "The decorating firm you've managed to drag through the gutter just by opening your big mouth, Davis."

"Oh, Lord," Paige moaned as Kellen took a step in Paul's direction. "Wait! Please don't do anything you'll regret later. Let's all sit down and—"

"I never mentioned your grand establishment, Martin," Kellen said, totally ignoring Paige's plea. "You can talk to the press if you're bugged about that. I'm concerned about Paige, but you obviously aren't."

"Like hell I'm not! I warned her about you from the beginning. You don't have any concept of what kind of woman Paige is. She needs protecting from men like you, Davis. You used her to further your sex image. From now on you keep away from her or—"

"Or what?" Kellen said, closing the distance between him and Paul in two long strides. "You'd better understand something, Martin. Paige is mine, and no flaky decorator is going to tell me—"

That did it! Paige's anger surfaced, and she let out a piercing scream that caused both men to stare at her in surprise. "You two overgrown playground bullies, get out of my house!" she yelled, pointing to the door. "I am not a bone to be haggled over. And for your information you both make me sick!"

"Now, Paige," Paul said, raising his hands in a quieting gesture.

"Out!" she said, deciding to stamp her foot after all. "Paul Martin, you had the audacity to come barreling in here and stand as judge and jury regarding my personal behavior. And you!" She turned to Kellen and poked him in the chest with her finger. "I do *not*—are you getting this?—I do *not* belong to you! You're a bum, Kellen Davis! You took what I thought was something special and turned it into a cheap headline. Don't open your mouths, either of you. Just pack it up and haul it out of here, or so help me, I'll call the police and have you thrown in jail!"

Kellen appeared as though he were about to say something, but as Paige squinted at him and folded her arms over her breasts in a defiant gesture, he turned and strode out of the apartment, slamming the door behind him.

"Paige," Paul said quietly, starting toward her.

"Out!"

"Dammit," he roared, exiting as loudly as Kellen had.

For the lack of something better to do, Paige stuck her tongue out at the door and then promptly burst into tears as she sank onto the sofa. *Now I've done it, but good,* she thought, a ragged sob escaping from her lips. Paul would fire her for sure and she couldn't blame him. And Kellen! The egotistical nerve of that man standing in her living room announcing that Paige Cunningham was his personal property. Ha! That would be the day! Well, she had shown those two that she couldn't be shoved around. Except, what was she going to do now? She was probably going to join the unemployed, and to top it off she'd threatened to have the man she loved thrown in the clink! Maybe she'd overplayed her tantrum a bit, but darn it, they had made her so mad!

"Men are ridiculous," she said, brushing the tears off her cheeks and marching into the kitchen for something to eat. "They're just little boys in grown-up bodies. I should have let them punch each other out."

An hour later Paige had eaten, taken a bath, and dressed in a fluffy robe. Her nerves were jangled, and she strained her ears for any sound in the corridor, fearing that Kellen or Paul might circle back for the last word. But all was silent and she finally crawled into bed in a state of exhaustion and fell immediately asleep.

A steady drumming noise brought her slowly awake, and she glanced foggily at the clock, seeing it was just after midnight. Sitting up in bed, she realized the continued thumping was coming from her front door, and switching on the bedroom light, she pulled on her robe and made her way cautiously across the living room.

"Who's there?" she called softly, her lips close to the door.

"Kellen," a voice mumbled.

"And Paul," another added.

Together? she thought wildly. Had they beaten each other up and come there for her to bandage their wounds? "What do you want?" she asked, her anger rising again.

"Got to talk to you," someone said not very clearly.

"Go away!" she said.

"No!" two voices said in unison.

"*Why me? Why me?*" she moaned, opening the door a crack, but keeping the chain firmly in place. She knew her mouth had dropped open, but she was unable to shut it as she peered out at the unbelievable scene before her. Kellen and Paul were standing together, not too steadily, each clutching a bedraggled bouquet of wilting flowers. Their hair was tousled, ties loosened, and the pungent aroma of liquor reached her nostrils.

"You're drunk!" she whispered.

"Very," Kellen said, his head bobbing strangely up and down.

"Gotta shpick, uh, speak to you," Paul slurred, after which a loud hiccup reverberated through the corridor. "My buddy here and I have somethin' to say."

Buddy? Paige thought. What was going on?

"What's all the noise?" a man yelled, poking his head out of a door.

"Oh, no." Paige closed the door and removed the

chain before quickly opening it again. "Get in here before we get arrested for disturbing the peace."

"Thank you," Kellen said formally as he stepped inside. He leaned back against the wall and pushed the flowers at her. "These are for you. Oops." He frowned as several blossoms dropped to the floor.

"These don't look so good," Paul said, peering at the bouquet in his hand before thrusting it in Paige's general direction.

"Sit down before you fall over," she said sharply, dumping the flowers on a chair and stepping back as the pair weaved their way to the sofa, where they landed heavily. "Now, do you suppose you two could explain this lovely visit?" she asked.

"Certainly," Kellen said, struggling to sit erect and then giving up the attempt.

"It's perfectly reasonable," Paul muttered, and then, as if in slow motion, he tipped over sideways on the cushion and closed his eyes.

"You see, Paige," Kellen began, but his voice trailed off as his long lashes fluttered and then lay still on his tanned cheeks.

"Hey!" Paige said, poking first Kellen and then Paul. "You can't pass out here! Wake up! I don't believe this!"

For several minutes Paige stood staring at the sleeping men. Then with a resigned sigh she tugged off their shoes and covered each with a spare blanket. A wave of tenderness brought a smile to her lips as she gently brushed Kellen's thick hair off his forehead. She gazed fondly at Paul, deciding he looked like a child after a hard day at play. She shook her head, then returned to her bed, where she pulled the covers up to her chin.

Wonders never cease, she thought, smiling into the darkness. She still said men were ridiculous but . . . dear. Lord knew how they'd ended up getting blitzed together. She wondered what they were going to say to her. The flowers were a sweet gesture. Maybe Paul wasn't going to fire her after all. And Kellen? Just what was Kellen trying to do?

Willing herself to relax, Paige burrowed deeper into the pillow. She was acutely aware that Kellen was only a few feet away from her and a wave of desire crept slowly through her body, her breasts throbbing with the remembrance of his tantalizing touch. Finally with a soft laugh she realized that even if she went into the other room and dragged Kellen into her bed, in the shape he was presently in he wouldn't even know it!

When the alarm went off the next morning, Paige shut it off quickly and hurried to the bedroom door and peered into the living room. Both Kellen and Paul were still sleeping soundly, and she grimaced when she saw the uncomfortable positions they had slumped into. Deciding it served them right if they couldn't walk straight for a week, she showered and dressed before setting a pot of coffee on to perk. She had taken one sip of the hot liquid when the telephone rang, and she dashed to answer it. Kellen moaned as she grabbed the receiver only inches from his head, but he didn't open his eyes.

"Yes?" she whispered.

"Paige? It's Timmy. I'm worried sick about Kellen. He was due on location at dawn. He has never done anything like this before. Not ever! I told him last night about your being upset about the television interview, and he left the set immediately to see you. Now this morning he's missing and—"

"Timmy, slow down," Paige said, her voice still hushed. "Kellen is sleeping off an overindulgence of alcohol. He's sprawled right here on my sofa with a man who has apparently become one of his best friends."

"Kellen got drunk? Drunk?" Timmy exclaimed.

"That's putting it mildly," Paige said, unable to suppress a smile.

"But he never does that!"

"Oh, no? Guess again. I have no idea when he'll wake up, and even then I have a hunch he won't feel up to being his charming self for the cameras."

"Wonderful," Timmy muttered. "I guess we'll shoot around him today."

"I'm leaving now to meet the painters at the house," Paige said. "Do you want to come collect this superior specimen?"

"I suppose I should. Who did you say was with him?"

"Paul Martin, my boss. You know, of the ever proper House of Martin?"

"Paul. . . . But Kellen grumbles that Martin might be a stumbling block between— This doesn't make sense. Of course, Kellen drinking too much and missing an early call is off the wall too. How did you get stuck with the dynamic duo?"

"It's a long story, Timmy. I'm going to hang up now because I have no desire to be here to witness the hangovers. I'll leave the door unlocked so you can get in and carry Mr. Davis away. There's a big pot of coffee in the kitchen if that will help."

"Bless you, child. You are a saint. I'm on my way."

"Good-bye, Timmy."

The sight of Scott Howlett and his crew waiting for her on the steps of Kellen's porch gave Paige a sense of reality. Since the midnight arrival of Kellen and Paul she had felt as though she were existing somewhere out in the middle of left field. In fact, she decided, she had seemed to enter a new and different world from the moment Kellen Davis had strode into her life.

She greeted Scott and unlocked the heavy doors to

the house. A delivery truck bringing the kitchen table and chairs arrived moments later, and Paige was delighted with the transformation of the sunny room once the picnic set had been banished to the back-yard. The odor of paint filled the downstairs, and she could almost picture the suffering Kellen turning green should Timmy elect to drag the patient home. Due to the fact that Kellen was not at his shining best and the workmen were in full attendance, Paige surmised that Timmy might hide Kellen out at the Camelback Inn until the star was human again.

As Paige gave the bookshelves a final inspection, she realized she was in a lighthearted mood. And she knew why. Kellen had obviously been trying to tell her something last night before he had passed out on her sofa. As stubborn as he was, she knew he would show up again on her doorstep to have his say. It didn't matter what the words were since they could change nothing, but she was guaranteed one last glimpse of him, and that made her eyes sparkle.

As he had done on numerous other jobs for Paige, Scott agreed to sign for any furniture deliveries that might arrive. Paige headed back into town and searched the shops for several hours before finding a good-sized Mexican rug that she could hang on Kellen's living-room wall. The tones matched the color scheme of the furniture and would add just the flair she was looking for. There was no doubt in her mind that the room would be ready for Kellen's Christmas party. The remainder of the items she had ordered would arrive today, and once the walls were painted, she would arrange everything and give it the finishing touch.

A sharp pain of depression struck her as she drove back to Kellen's in the late afternoon. When she had completed her job of decorating, she would have no excuse to wander through Kellen's home. She would hand back the key and walk away forever.

Scott had received the delivery of several lamps and tables and had carefully covered each with drop cloths. The room was taking shape beautifully, and Paige was pleased with the one wall she had chosen to be done in a light cocoa color to offset the white of the others that would be painted next.

"TGIF," Scott said, popping a lid onto a bucket of paint. "I'm going to put my feet up and not move all weekend. I won't ask you what you're going to do because you'll say it's none of my business, so good night, so long, see you on Monday, and all that good stuff, Paige."

"Have a nice couple of days," she said.

Paige stood alone in the large quiet room, imagining how splendid it would be when it was finally completed. Christmas would come, and Kellen would throw open the doors to receive his guests. But despite her agreement to stay with him through the holidays, she knew she could no longer do that. She would see him once more to hear the explanation he seemed so determined to give and then say good-bye for the last time. She closed the door behind her, locked it securely, and drove slowly back into town.

Riding up in the elevator in her building, she had the sudden thought that Paul had better not be camped out in her apartment. She knew Timmy would have removed the ailing Kellen Davis, and Paul Martin better be off the premises as well. She was in no mood to see either of the midnight prowlers, and they both would be long gone if they knew what was good for them!

A note taped to her door from the manager saying he had allowed a delivery to be made piqued her curiosity, and she quickly entered, then gasped as she unsteadily closed the door behind her. Her apartment looked like a dry run for the Rose Bowl parade. There were bouquets of flowers everywhere in every color imaginable, and the fragrances were heavenly. Paige stepped through the pretty jungle until she located a white card tucked among some red roses. It read *I'm sorry.—Kellen.*

"Oh, Kellen," she whispered. "Sorry for what? Arriving on my doorstep dead drunk? Sorry for what you said on television? Sorry you ever met me? It doesn't matter anyway. We never had a chance."

The blankets sat neatly folded on the sofa, and in the kitchen the coffeepot and mugs were washed and in the drainer. Mentally thanking Timmy for his thoughtfulness, Paige ate a light supper and then gingerly made her way through the bouquets to indulge in a leisurely bubble bath. After she pinned her hair on top of her head, she sank into the soothing water up to her chin, instantly smacking her hand against the tile wall in annoyance as a sharp knock sounded at the front door.

"Now what?" she fumed, stepping out of the tub and wrapping a towel around her body. "Whoever it is, I don't want any."

She ran to the door, leaving wet tracks on the carpet. "Come back later or something," she yelled through the panel.

"Paige? It's Kellen. May I come in?"

Kellen! Here? Now? she thought frantically, glancing down at the scanty towel she was clutching around herself. She thought he'd still be moaning and groaning with a headache.

"Paige? Please. Open the door."

"Why not?" she muttered in defeat, throwing it open and waving him in.

"Hi," he said, grinning rather sheepishly. "Like the flowers?"

"They're lovely. Thank you," she said, totally aware

he was his usual gorgeous self and looked no worse for wear in tight faded jeans and a brown velour sweater. "I'm freezing to death, Kellen. What is it you wanted?"

"You," he said, his voice low and husky. "I want you, Paige Cunningham."

Seven

Paige could feel her heart start to race as she gazed up into Kellen's sapphire-blue eyes, which were growing cloudy with desire.

"Just like that?" she snapped, pulling the towel more tightly into place. "After everything you've done, you just waltz in here and announce you want me? Lord, Kellen, you've got a lot of nerve."

"True," he said seriously. "But I'm honest," he added, grinning at her.

"Honest!" Paige gasped, her eyes widening. "You don't know the meaning of the word! You've lived in a fantasy world for so long, Kellen, you can't decipher between what's real and what isn't."

"Paige, please let me explain," he said, raking his hand through his hair. "But put some clothes on before I go crazy."

"Brother," she said, heading for the bedroom and nearly tripping over a big bunch of yellow mums. She emerged moments later, completely covered in her fluffy robe. Standing across the room from Kellen, she folded her arms over her breasts. "Well?" she asked coolly.

"Come sit down," he said, gesturing toward the sofa.

Why was she being so bitchy? she wondered, but still scowled as she plunked herself down on the sofa. Because it was keeping her from running into Kellen's arms, that's why. This was the speech she knew he wanted to give, and it was her final chance to see him. She wouldn't make a fool of herself by falling apart and begging him to hold her just one last time. She loved him, but he'd never, never know.

"Paige?"

"Pardon? Oh, yes, Kellen."

"Will you listen to me? Really listen?" he asked, sitting down next to her.

"I don't think you have anything to say that I want to hear," she said, smoothing the material of her robe, "but since you're so determined, go ahead."

"You're not planning to make this easy for me, are you?"

"Should I?" she asked, looking at him steadily. *I should get an Oscar for this performance*, she told herself. She was really coming across as an honest-to-goodness shrew!

"No, I deserve every bit of your anger and mistrust in me," he said softly, resting his elbows on his knees and clasping his hands together.

"You do?" she whispered.

"Paige, when that reporter shoved that microphone in my face, I reacted automatically. I pushed the button that activated Kellen Davis the sex symbol and said everything that was expected of me. I really didn't give it much thought. The minute the cameras stopped rolling, I rebuttoned my shirt, put the interview out of my mind, and went back to trying to produce a movie."

"Lovely," Paige muttered.

"Timmy came bustling up to me right away all in a dither. He said I should never have implied what I did. He felt that by my making those suggestive remarks about you, I had placed our relationship in jeopardy."

"Timmy is a wise man," she said quietly.

"I just waved him off. I told him that you understood that I had an image to maintain and there wasn't a problem. After I spoke with the reporter, Felicia kind of slithered up and wrapped herself around me to make it look good. She knew what game we were playing, and I assumed you would too. I was wrong, Paige, very, very wrong. It wasn't until Timmy told me that you were upset that I even knew I had made a mistake."

"Kellen . . ."

"Paige, for the first time since I can remember I took a long look at myself and believe me, I didn't like what I saw. You are the finest thing that has happened to me in my life and what we've shared is more precious than I can say. But when it got right down to it, I didn't know how to handle something as beautiful and rare as what we have. The first time the public wanted me to perform I used you to further my own image. I can't forgive myself for that. I really can't."

"Oh, Kellen." Paige reached out and rested her hand lightly on his back.

Kellen turned and looked at her, a haunting pain crossing his face as he gazed at her. Their eyes met and held, and with a slight shudder Kellen pushed himself to his feet, staring down at her from his lofty height.

"Paige," he said, taking a shaking breath, "when you threw Paul and me out of here last night, I didn't know what to do. I was frantic, afraid you'd never speak to me again. Paul was in the same shape. He was scared to death you'd quit the House of Martin and tell him where to put himself. He considers you a dear friend, and he was convinced you'd shoot him on sight the next time you saw him. The two of us stood out in the hall feeling sorry for ourselves and ended up going off together to drown our sorrows."

"Do tell," she said, shaking her head at the memory of their midnight arrival at her door.

"Needless to say, we were in no shape to apologize when we came here, but it sure seemed like a good idea at the time. The next thing I knew, Timmy was hauling me off to his room at the Camelback Inn, calling me every name in the book. He tossed Paul out while he was at it too. Paul's a good man, but he qualifies for the Fool of the Year Award right along with me."

"I'm sure you and Paul suffered enough from the aftereffects of your grand night without me giving you a lecture, Kellen. Let's just forget it."

"Paige, my getting drunk is not the point here. It's much more than that. I'm asking you to forgive me for not having the intelligence or the depth of feeling to realize that I couldn't treat you and our relationship in the manner that I did. I'll make it up to you, Paige, if you'll only give me a chance. Please let me back into your world. Don't sentence me to a lonely, empty Christmas without you because I'm an idiot. I know what I did was wrong, but I didn't set out to intentionally hurt you or to destroy . . . us. I said I wanted you, Paige, but it's more than that. I need you, and there's a big difference between the two."

Paige lowered her eyes to conceal the hot tears that were threatening to spill over onto her cheeks. Kellen was saying everything she could possibly wish to hear. The ultimate joy would be if he loved her, but she really didn't expect that. He was totally aware of what he had done and sorry for his thoughtless actions. Kellen wanted her and, dear God, needed her. The pain in his eyes was real, raw, and her heart ached with love for this giant of a man who stood before her, asking for her forgiveness and renewed trust. They could have their Christmas together, after all. It was up to her. She had neither the strength nor the desire to walk away from him. Not now. Not yet.

"Kellen," she said, getting up and standing before him. "The next time you apologize, do you think you could refrain from turning my living room into a funeral parlor?"

"Paige . . ."

"Kellen," she said, taking a deep breath, "I have something I want to say. I'm guilty of things too. When I first met you, I responded to you in a manner that shocked and embarrassed me. But then, Kellen, I used you."

"No, Paige—"

"I did! I realized that you were capable of making me finally let go of Jerry's ghost. You awakened the woman in me and brought such joy to my life. I took from you, Kellen, not even knowing if I was giving you anything meaningful in return. I was selfish and self-centered because all I knew was that I felt alive again. But then it began to have greater meaning to me. I care deeply for you, Kellen, and now I must ask your forgiveness for not being completely honest with you in the beginning. You were a tool to rid myself of Jerry, and that wasn't fair. If you still want to, Kellen, we'll have the most wonderful Christmas imaginable."

"Oh, Paige," Kellen moaned, pulling her roughly into his arms. "Oh, my Paige. I knew Jerry was standing between us. Why do you think I worked so hard to rid you of him? You didn't use me, Paige. I understood what you had to do. But now you're free. Free to come to me, if you will. Say it, Paige, please. Let me hear that you forgive me."

"Oh, Kellen, I do. I want you and I need you. We'll close the door on the world again and—"

"No," he said, taking her by the shoulders and looking deep into her eyes. "We tried that before and it didn't work. It's too big out there, Paige, and the world has a way of sneaking in and leaving its mark on us. We'll meet it head-on together and see what happens. No more hiding. You are my lady and that's how it's going to be. We'll face each day as it comes. Just don't leave me."

"I'm here, Kellen," she whispered. For now, my darling, she thought. For our merry Christmas, I'm here.

Kellen drew her close and held her, not moving, hardly breathing, as if she were made of the finest china that might crumble and disappear in a wispy cloud of dust. Slowly he reached up and pulled the pins from her hair, his long fingers releasing the heavy tresses so they fell past her shoulders. Paige looked up into his smoldering eyes, her heart beating erratically in anticipation of what would come.

She's mine, Kellen thought fiercely. *Paige is mine!* He'd never hurt her again. He'd been so empty when he'd felt she didn't want or need him anymore. But now she was back in his arms and he was not going to let her go!

"Kellen?" Paige whispered. "Is something wrong?"

"No. Oh, no, Paige, everything is very right."

In a long warm, tender embrace he kissed her. And she responded, blinking back tears of joy as she wrapped her arms around his waist and spread her fingers across his broad back. The kiss intensified, kindling the embers of passion until they burst into a roaring flame. Kellen pushed the robe off her shoulders, his lips and tongue flickering over her breasts as they came into view. She trembled, hardly able to stand as a soft moan escaped from her lips.

"Kellen, please," she said, taking a shaking breath. "Come to my room. Love me, Kellen, and then hold me all night in your arms."

Together they moved through the bouquets of fragrant flowers, their hands clasped tightly. In the bedroom Paige dropped the robe to the floor and swept back the blankets on the bed as Kellen quickly shed his clothes. They stood several feet apart, each gazing at the beauty of the other, allowing the desire to build, to run rampant within them, knowing their journey together would bring only ecstasy and magnificent fulfillment to their aching bodies. The sheets were cool against their shimmering skin as they lay close—touching, kissing, rediscovering all there was to know of the other's mysteries. Through the night they reached for each other, quelling over and over the burning heat of desire that was never totally extinguished. They dozed lightly, neither wishing to end their hours of bliss until, finally spent and contented, they fell into a quiet slumber entwined in each other's arms.

Paige woke to find her head resting on Kellen's shoulder and gazed up at his handsome face, seeing the thick lashes lying against his tanned cheeks. As a slow smile crept onto the corners of his mouth, she laughed aloud. "You're faking," she said, poking him in the chest. "I know you're awake."

"I was waiting to see if you'd try to seduce me while I was sleeping," he said, chuckling softly, his blue eyes clear and sparkling.

"After last night? Goodness, Kellen, are you Superman in disguise?"

"Try me," he said, reaching up and running his hand down her side.

"Oh!" Paige gasped, suddenly sitting bolt up in the bed. "What time is it? Don't you have to be on the movie set?"

"It's Saturday, remember?"

"I know, but you missed yesterday, and I thought—"

"I'm not having my crew come in on their day off because I was a naughty boy and didn't show when I was supposed to. The weekend is ours. Hey, let's go Christmas shopping."

"But you'll be recognized everywhere we go."

"And I'll sign the autographs like a dutiful star and we'll move on," he said quietly, stroking her back. "We're not camping out here just because we might have to share a little of our time with the public. Okay, my lady?"

"All right, Kellen." She smiled as she looked down at him. "I guess I can handle all those women drooling over you. Just don't bring any of them home."

"Gee, you're no fun," he complained, pushing himself off the bed. "Let's shower, eat, and go spend gobs of money. Oh, and another thing. We wrap the stuff ourselves. We'll get paper and tags and bows and—"

"Yes! Yes! Yes!" She laughed. "Quit talking and move it, Davis. Time is wasting."

They devoured huge plates full of scrambled eggs and toast while Kellen chattered on about the fabulous time they were going to have shopping for gifts. His enthusiasm was infectious, and when he smiled at her, Paige couldn't help but return the expression. She was loading the dishwasher when the telephone rang. Calling to Kellen to answer it, she soon heard his rich, throaty laughter coming from the living room.

"That was Paul," he said a few minutes later as he entered the kitchen. "He wanted to know if it was safe to come out of hiding. I told him you had mercy and had decided not to murder us."

"I did? I thought maybe I'd still think it over for a while."

"I'll ignore that remark. Listen, Paige, on Monday we're doing some scenes on the Arizona State University campus and I wondered if you'd like to come over and watch."

"I'd love to, but I have to work."

"I'm one step ahead of you. I invited Paul too. He said you should take the day off."

"But I have to meet Scott Howlett, the painter, out at your house at nine to let him in."

"Timmy will do that."

"But—"

"Don't you want to see me in action?" Kellen smiled an endearing little-boy smile.

"Of course, I do. It sounds like fun."

"Good. Ready to leave?"

"Just about." Oh, dear, she thought, she wasn't sure about this. Talk about walking smack-dab into the middle of Kellen's world. Why couldn't they close the door on the whole thing as they had before? He was so insistent now that they march right out there and tackle it head-on. She wasn't sure she wanted to!

Pushing aside her distressing thoughts, Paige grabbed her sweater and they dashed from the apartment out into the crisp, clear day. Twenty minutes later they were caught up in the throngs of people at a large shopping mall. Christmas carols danced through the air, and the store windows were bursting with vibrant colors and exquisite displays.

Kellen bought an expensive briefcase of the finest leather for Timmy and passed judgment on the silk scarves Paige spread out on the counter before deciding on one for her to give to Janet. She selected an unusual paperweight for Paul, and Kellen got his newfound buddy a gold pen-and-pencil set. She wanted to give Timmy a gift, but didn't wish to embarrass the older man. Kellen insisted Timmy would be sincerely touched and she settled for a pair of driving gloves. They loaded up on paper and bows and tags and were laughing merrily as they maneuvered their bundles through the crowds.

"Kellen Davis!" a voice suddenly screamed. "It's Kellen Davis!"

Here we go, folks, Paige thought gloomily as she saw heads turn and women, girls, and even a few men, converge on them.

"Hello," Kellen said, smiling at the group.

"May I have your autograph, Mr. Davis?" a squeaky voice pleaded.

"Well, I don't exactly have a free hand here," he said, glancing down at the packages in his arms.

"Set them down. I'll watch them," Paige said quietly.

"Oh!" a woman said. "You're not Felicia Evans, so you must be Paige Cunningham. May I have your autograph too, Miss Cunningham?"

"Pardon me?" Paige asked, her eyes wide.

"I'll tell you what," Kellen said. "We'll sign them together. As a couple."

"Felicia's going to love this," someone giggled.

"Felicia and I have been friends for a long time," Kellen said seriously. "I'm afraid there's been a misunderstanding regarding our relationship. She's like a sister to me. We've shared a lot and we're very close but, ladies, Felicia Evans and I have never been lovers. I think it's time that was made perfectly clear."

Dear heaven, Paige thought wildly, what was he doing? He was blowing his image right out of the window!

"Then you and Miss Cunningham . . ." a woman started to say.

"We'll be happy to sign your autographs together. Okay?" Kellen flashed one of his most engaging smiles. Had he actually said all that about Felicia? he thought, shaking his head slightly. Well, dammit, he had to! He couldn't stand there with Paige right next to him and insinuate again that he was bouncing back and forth between her and Felicia. These women sure didn't seem to care that he and Felicia were just friends.

"Mine first, Mr. Davis," a woman called, shoving a piece of paper at him, "but please leave room for Miss Cunningham to sign."

Kellen turned to Paige, a questioning look on his face. He let out an audible sigh of relief as he saw the warm smile on her lips. For the next fifteen minutes the pair scribbled their names on shopping lists, paper bags, anything, and then Kellen glanced at his watch. He loudly remembered an appointment he had to keep, collected their packages, and hustled Paige away from the crowd.

After stowing their treasures in the trunk of the car they sank onto the plush seats. Neither spoke for several minutes.

"Kellen," Paige finally said quietly, "why did you do that? By telling the truth about your relationship with Felicia, you've certainly done damage to yourself."

Kellen turned and laid his arm across the top of the seat. "Paige, I wasn't about to humiliate you again. I wanted it clear that we were together, and it wasn't because you'd drawn the lucky number today."

"But—"

"I don't think you understand. I told you I wouldn't hurt you anymore and I intend to keep that promise. If some of my fans don't like me being a straight arrow then that's just tough."

"You're not using your head," she said, her voice

rising slightly. "You're doing things now that are going to have far-reaching effects. When you leave Phoenix and go back to California, you won't be able to repair the—"

"What are you saying?" Kellen asked, his jaw tightening.

"You don't live here, Kellen," Paige said softly. "You know that."

"Oh? And what is that place you're decorating for me? A hotel?" he snapped.

"What are you going to do?" she yelled. "Make your next ten movies in Arizona? Don't be ridiculous. When you've finished this film, you'll leave. You'll be gone, Kellen, and that will be that. We agreed to spend Christmas together, but I have no illusions about the future because we don't have one!"

"Is that what this is to you, Paige?" Kellen growled. "A holiday fling?"

"Damn you! Don't you dare insinuate such a thing. I'll cherish every moment we share and you know it. But I'm being realistic, Kellen. Oh, this conversation is crazy!"

"This conversation," Kellen said, forcefully turning the key in the ignition, "is over!"

Paige opened her mouth to protest when she saw that Kellen was driving in the direction of his house rather than her apartment, then decided to forget it. As stubborn as he was, he'd take her wherever he pleased anyway. He was acting so strangely. It was as though he were burying his head in the sand and pretending they were a normal couple with the delicious luxury of planning beyond tomorrow; that simply was not true. She believed in him now, knew for certain that he cared for her, but nothing could change the facts. What did he propose she do? Toss aside her career and become his mistress, following him around the universe holed up in hotel rooms while he went off to flex his muscles in front of the camera? Their worlds did not mesh. They had nothing in common except the glow of happiness that surrounded them when they were together. It sounded romantic, but it wasn't enough to build a lifetime on.

"Kellen, don't be so crabby," she said suddenly, surprising herself at her cross remark.

"Well, hell!" he snapped. "You act as though you plan to pack me away with the Christmas decorations and forget me!"

"Now that," she said, bursting into laughter, "was funny!"

"Darn it, Paige," he said, smiling in spite of himself, "would you be serious?"

"No, I refuse. We had a marvelous morning shopping, and I signed autographs just like a very important person and it was fun and now I'm hungry."

"Okay, okay." He chuckled. "We'll call a truce. Just bear in mind that my makeup man is not going to appreciate it if you give me my first gray hair."

"Tsk, tsk," she clucked. "That would be a rotten shame."

"Woman, you are going to get it," he said, waggling a finger at her.

"I certainly hope so," she said, batting her eyelashes at him, which brought a whoop of laughter from Kellen.

Kellen's living room was so cluttered that they wrapped their packages sitting on the floor of the large empty den on the other side of the entry hall. Kellen proved to be an expert at making bows, and Paige was quite happy to assign him that job. They ate as they worked, consuming ham-and-cheese sandwiches and ice-cold soda. They squabbled over the scissors, Paige accused Kellen of not sharing the roll of tape, and he tied her finger tightly inside a red ribbon when she volunteered to hold it in place. They had an absolutely wonderful time.

Later, Kellen built a fire in the living room and, ignoring the debris, they sat in front of the crackling flames and reread the beautiful book about Christmas. The hours passed and they raided the refrigerator again. As the last glow of the fire died away into graying embers, they climbed the stairs and through the glorious night traveled over and over to their private place of ecstasy.

"You know," Paige said thoughtfully the next morning as she sipped a cup of coffee, "we're not very organized. One of us ends up wearing the same clothes two days in a row."

"So move in here," Kellen said, popping some bread into the toaster.

"Are you kidding? Your living room is a mess."

"The bedroom is neat as a pin though."

"True, but I still think I'll pass on the offer, thanks."

"Why?" Kellen asked, suddenly serious as he turned to look at her.

"Don't be silly." She frowned and took a hasty drink of her coffee.

"Think about it," he said, turning to retrieve the toast. "I happen to consider it a terrific idea."

"Pay attention, Kellen. I am now changing the subject. What would you like to do today?"

"Loaded question."

"I was referring to an outdoor activity."

"Oh. Well, how about going for a nice long drive where there are absolutely no people."

"And desert my fans for an entire day? Really, Kellen, how thoughtless."

"I've created a monster."

"A drive sounds lovely," she said. "Just peace and quiet, thee and me."

"Now you're catching on. Here, eat some toast."

* * *

Late that night Paige smiled into the darkness as she lay in bed in her apartment. She clutched the pillow that still held the lingering aroma of Kellen and thought back over the delightful day that had ended in their making love after returning to Paige's. They had driven for hours, heading nowhere in particular as they explored the back roads of the Phoenix area. They had enjoyed a picnic in a shady grove of mesquite trees and walked over the desert terrain, enjoying the unique sights and sounds.

It had been so peaceful and comfortable as they chatted about their childhood days, revealed forgotten hopes and dreams, and told tales of silly and embarrassing events in their lives. They had touched and kissed in the sunshine, held hands, and had a foot race to a distant boulder that Paige miraculously won. Tired but happy, they had returned to town, where they ate soggy tacos in the car before joining in simultaneous yawns. Kellen had given Paige passes to allow her and Paul on the movie set the next morning.

Kellen had tugged on his clothes despite Paige's urgings that he stay the night. He had a camera call at dawn and insisted she needed a good night's sleep for a change. His parting kiss had been long and powerful, almost causing him to change his mind.

A lovely weariness consumed Paige, and she sighed contentedly. The day had been perfect. Nothing and no one had interrupted her time with Kellen. He had been attentive and fun and wonderful. He had been hers alone, and the hours in his protective care had reaffirmed again and again in her heart how much she loved him. Tomorrow she would watch him performing in his life's work. And the tomorrows after that? They were few, but tonight she wouldn't dwell on it. She was too happy, too full of inner peace and joy to allow anything to tarnish it.

"Good night, Kellen," she said to no one. "I love you. Be it right or wrong, I love you."

The next morning as Paige entered the House of Martin she had the strange sensation that it had been an eternity since she had been there. So much had happened in her previously quiet and well-ordered life in such a short time, and she felt ridiculously relieved when Janet called her by name and wished her the usual good morning.

"Here," Paige said, plunking a large vase of carnations in the middle of Janet's desk, "have a flower."

"They're beautiful," Janet gushed. "Am I celebrating something?"

"Well, you see, Mr. Davis got a little carried away in a florist's shop and I thought I'd share the wealth."

"Kellen Davis ordered *these*?" Janet shrieked. "He opened his mouth and spoke of these very carnations? Did he see them?"

"Yes, he came by after—"

"Those blue eyes have gazed upon these blossoms, leaves, and stems? Oh, Mrs. Cunningham! Thank you! I'll keep them for life. I'll throw my body in front of them to keep human hands from touching them. I'll—"

"My goodness," Paige muttered, walking away as Janet continued to ramble on.

"Paige!" Paul called, coming down the corridor to meet her.

"Hi, Paul." She smiled at him. "You're looking . . . fit."

"Please," he moaned. "Don't mention the other night except to say you accept my apology. I have never been so hung over in my life. Only good thing that came of the fiasco was that I had an opportunity to get to know Kellen. Helluva guy. I really like him,

Paige. He can't hold his liquor any better than I can, but he's a good man."

"I know," Paige said softly.

"Hey, what's this?" he said, tilting her chin up and studying her face. "Is there a glow on those cheeks? A sparkle in the big brown eyes? Yep. You've gone and done it, haven't you?"

"Done what?"

"Fallen in love with Kellen Davis," Paul said, smiling at her warmly.

"I— No, of course not. He— I mean— Well—"

"I'm happy for you, sweetheart. I really am. It was time, Paige, and you made a fine choice. Kellen is the real goods."

"Paul, please," she said, shaking her head miserably, "don't. You're my dear friend and I can't hide anything from you nor do I want to. But, Paul, it's not how you think. I'll admit only to you that I'm in love with Kellen, but he doesn't know it and—"

"Come into my office," he interrupted, grabbing her by the arm and literally hauling her down the hall. "Now," he said, shutting the door and motioning her into a chair. "What's all this garbage about not telling Kellen how you feel?"

"Paul, what Kellen and I have is beautiful. Special. Rare. But it's temporary, and I know that. It would serve no purpose to complicate things by making a grand declaration of my love. Nothing would change."

"Color me dense, Paige, but I don't understand. I got blitzed with that man the other night, remember? You were the only one he talked about. He cares very deeply for you, I'm sure of it."

"Oh, Paul, I know that. I trust and believe in Kellen. Every time I say the slightest thing about our relationship ending soon, he gets very upset, angry. But one of us has to be realistic. Deep inside he knows it's hopeless, but he's pretending we'll ride off into the sunset together or some insane thing."

"Why? Why can't you and Kellen make it?" Paul said, throwing up his hands.

"My God, Paul, think about it!" Paige said, getting to her feet. "Just because I love Kellen doesn't mean I could function in his world. There's nothing for me there. He belongs to his public. Everywhere we go, they fawn over him, demand his time and attention. He isn't free, Paul, not really."

"Paige, when two people are in love, they find a way to—"

"Kellen has never said he loves me, Paul," Paige said quietly.

"He—"

"But it doesn't matter, don't you see? I've been so happy with him, so alive. I've buried Jerry's ghost and learned to laugh again. I'll cry when he leaves me, Paul, but then I'll dry the tears and hold each memory of my moments with him in my heart forever."

"Paige, this is crazy! Tell the man you love him, for Pete's sake. He has a right to know. He deserves the chance to—"

"No," she said firmly. "I'm not doing anything to ruin the time I have left with him, Paul. It's getting late. Let's go over to the campus before we miss everything."

"Yeah. Okay," Paul muttered, following her from the room.

"Oh, Mr. Martin," Janet said as Paige and Paul walked by, "did you see my flowers? They're from Kellen Davis! Well, not exactly, but he was in the same room with them and—"

Paul laughed. "Very nice. I'll tell you what. Mrs. Cunningham and I will tell Mr. Davis what a devoted fan you are and see about getting you his autograph."

"Really?" The girl gasped, placing her hand over her heart. "Really? Really?"

"Really!" Paige and Paul said in unison as they left the office.

The Arizona State University campus was teeming with people, some scurrying to classes while another huge crowd stood behind a roped-off area, craning their necks in the hopes of getting a glimpse of the movie stars. Kellen had given Paul instructions to come to the majestic Frank Lloyd Wright Auditorium where the scene was to be shot, and to show the passes to one of the security guards that lined the restricted area.

Paige felt a tingle of excitement rush over her as they inched their way through the throng. She had chosen a simple lime-green wool dress for the occasion and had brushed her hair into a shiny cascade. She knew her eyes were sparkling as she smiled up at Paul, who kept a firm grip on her elbow. The guard nodded them through, which brought whispers of speculation from those behind them as to who they were. There was a multitude of equipment in the area, and Paige and Paul stepped carefully over the heavy cables as they cautiously made their way forward.

"Paige! Paige! Over here!" a voice called.

"Felicia!" Paige said, grabbing Paul's arm and pulling him toward the smiling woman. "How nice to see you again."

"I'm so glad you're here," Felicia said.

"Felicia, I'd like you to meet my boss, Paul Martin."

"Miss Evans," Paul said, his gaze seeming to be glued to the pretty actress's face.

"Ah-ha!" Felicia laughed. "You're the other half of the drunk-as-a-skunk team. You and Kellen are dangerous together."

"We . . . overestimated our capacity." Paul grinned sheepishly.

"You men can be such absurd creatures at times," Felicia said, "but your sexiness makes up for it. Paige, Kellen will be here in a minute. He's checking some technical junk. Ever since he started his own company, he's so very, very serious about all that stuff."

"Makeup please, Miss Evans," a man called.

"Coming, Mickey! Paige, Paul, I'll see you after we shoot the scene," Felicia said as she hurried away.

"Lord," Paul whispered.

"Problem?" Paige asked.

"That has got to be the most gorgeous woman I have seen in my entire life."

"Well, thanks a bunch!"

"Huh? Oh, sorry, Paige, I didn't mean that you aren't."

"Relax." Paige laughed. "I know she's beautiful. She's also very friendly and, well, human. There's nothing phoney about Felicia Evans."

"You mean everything in that sweater is real too?"

"Paul!"

"Just thought I'd ask. Hey, there's Kellen."

Paige could hear a buzz of excitement ripple through the crowd as Kellen approached. Clad in black pants that hugged his taut legs and a black silk shirt open to midchest, he looked devastating.

Sorry, y'all, she thought merrily. *For now, he's mine!*

"Hi, babe," Kellen said, smiling at Paige after nodding to Paul.

"Hi," she said, her eyes glowing.

"Excuse me, buddy," Kellen said to Paul, "but I really need to kiss my lady."

"Be my guest," Paul said, grinning.

Before Paige could decide if it was a good idea,

Kellen had cupped her face in his large hands and was kissing her passionately as the spectators cheered.

"I feel better now," Kellen said when he finally released her.

"If I'm blushing, don't tell me," Paige said. "I don't want to know."

"Kellen," Felicia said, coming to join them, "they're ready for us."

"Paige, move up closer," Kellen said, "so you can see better. Paul, take her over there by that crane."

"Say, Paul," Felicia said, "want to help the cause?"

"The what?" Paul asked.

"Kellen is trying very hard to undo the damage he did on that television interview the other night. That crowd just saw him kiss Paige, and all their beady little eyes are waiting for my reaction. Now if they thought that you and I . . . But I guess that's a bad plan. I mean, you do have your reputation to think of."

"Never let it be said that Paul Martin didn't come to the aid of his friends," Paul said, his grin belying his chivalrous tone.

As Paige's eyes widened in shock Paul gathered Felicia into his arms and kissed her so enthusiastically, Paige was sure they'd have to call for an oxygen tank. The crowd went wild, applauding and cheering them on. Kellen's throaty chuckle reached Paige's ears, and she looked up in time to receive a wink from a sapphire-blue eye.

"How did I do?" Paul asked finally, close to Felicia's lips.

"Fantastic," Felicia whispered. "I like you, Paul Martin."

"I hate to break this up," Kellen said, shaking his head and grinning, "but some of us have to earn a living around here."

"Go away, Kellen," Felicia said absently, making no attempt to move out of Paul's arms.

"She's at the Camelback Inn, Paul," Kellen said, disengaging Felicia and propelling her in the direction she needed to go. "Call her."

"Right." Paul nodded, his eyes appearing slightly glassy.

"It's going to be in the newspapers, you know," Paige said as she and Paul walked to where Kellen had indicated they could obtain the best view. "That was a dumb thing to do, Paul."

"That, my child, was the smartest thing I have ever done. Incredible woman, that Felicia. I have been kissed in my day, but never like that! Definitely going to give the lady a call."

Paige laughed. "Oh, my."

"Quiet on the set, please," a man boomed out over a bullhorn. "I want complete quiet on the set."

Paige watched spellbound as a door of the auditorium opened and Kellen glanced out cautiously as if making sure no one was around. Reaching behind him, he pulled Felicia forward and then flattened her against the wall by pressing his hand on her stomach. The expression on Felicia's face was of utter terror, and Paige gasped softly at the transformation that had come over the actress.

Slowly, steadily, Kellen inched them along the balcony, their backs rigid against the bricks. Kellen's eyes darted back and forth, his jaw set in a tight hard line. Every inch of his body seemed coiled, ready to pounce at the slightest provocation. Hardly breathing, Paige covered her cheeks with her hands, her eyes never leaving the tension-packed scene before her.

Suddenly a man crept toward the building, moving swiftly in the grass as he hunched over, keeping out of Kellen's line of vision. With agonizing slowness the man drew a large gun from inside his coat, gripped it with both hands, and began inching toward Kellen and Felicia.

"KELLEN!" Paige screamed at the top of her lungs. "Watch out! He's got a gun and he's going to kill you! Kellen!"

Eight

"Oh, my God," Paige whispered. "What have I done?"

She had created a bedlam, to be precise. Cameramen, technicians, literally everyone seemed to be hollering at once. A man jumped out of a canvas chair and ferociously threw a clipboard to the ground. The crowd of spectators buzzed with confusion while the person with the bullhorn demanded they be quiet. Paul stared at Paige with his mouth open as if he had never seen her before in his life.

And Kellen? He slowly slid down the wall and landed on his bottom with a thud, wrapping his arms around his stomach and laughing so uproariously he could hardly catch his breath. The sound was infectious and Felicia immediately fell apart, joining Kellen on the floor and whooping with merriment until tears ran down her cheeks.

"I want to go home," Paige said weakly, but no one paid any attention to her.

Struggling for air, Kellen pushed himself to his feet

and sprinted over to where Paige was standing. She covered her face with her hands, having the wildly irrational thought that if she didn't look at him he'd forget that she was there.

"Paige," he gasped, pulling her hands away and tilting her chin up with one finger.

"Oh, Kellen, I'm so sorry. It's just that when I saw that man . . . He had a gun and you didn't know he was there and— I'm so, so sorry! I've never been more frightened in my life and—"

"You are wonderful," he said, chuckling as he pulled her into his arms and rested his chin on the top of her head. "Absolutely, totally fabulous."

"But I ruined everything," she said miserably into his shirt.

"Paige, are you all right?" Felicia asked breathlessly as she joined them. "Paul, close your mouth."

"Oh," Paul said as if coming out of a trance.

"She's fine," Kellen said. "We just shook her up a little. One thing is for sure, Felicia, we don't have to worry about whether or not that scene creates the tension we want. It definitely passed the test."

"I'm so sorry," Paige mumbled.

"Now!" Kellen pulled back and gazed down at Paige. "Do you think you're up to watching it again? Remember, I'm the hero. That guy can't kill me, it's against the rules."

"Yes, okay." She nodded obediently. "I won't say a word. I promise."

"All right, you people," a man bellowed. "Is this nonsense over with? Mickey, check their makeup. I want a take this time!"

Paige clenched her jaw tightly as the scene was re-enacted, Paul giving her a warning look as the villain advanced toward the building. Suddenly, with lightning speed, Kellen leaped into action and kicked the gun out of the bad guy's fist. Paige was about to yell "Hurray!" when Paul clamped his hand over her mouth and kept it there until a man hollered, "Cut!"

"I swear, Paige," Paul grumbled, "you're going to put me in an early grave. You nearly blew it again."

"But it was so exciting! Did you see Kellen? Pow! That nasty man never had a chance."

"Everyone survive?" Kellen asked when he and Felicia joined them.

"Oh, Kellen," Paige said, her eyes dancing with excitement, "that was unbelievable. You were marvelous! I'm so proud of you. I bet that crumb won't try to put one over on you again."

Kellen laughed. "Sure he will. Only next time he uses a knife."

"Oh, dear." She frowned. "That hardly seems fair."

"Well," Felicia said, "I'm finished for today. We've been here since the crack of dawn, and I don't have any more scenes scheduled until tomorrow. What about you, Kellen?"

"I have a production meeting that will take up the afternoon."

"In that case, Paige," Felicia said, "why don't you and I go shopping for new dresses for Kellen's Christmas bash? That is, if your handsome boss here will give you the rest of the day off."

"Sure," Paul said, his head bobbing up and down as he gazed at Felicia.

"Say, Paul," Felicia said, smiling enchantingly, "how's this for pushy? Would you like to take me to Kellen's Christmas party?"

"I—I'd be delighted," Paul stammered.

"Super. Kellen, kiss Paige good-bye so we can get on with our shopping spree."

"I always do as I'm told," Kellen said before kissing Paige deeply, leaving her knees feeling as wobbly as gelatin. "I'll call you later," he said when he finally lifted his head and smiled at her tenderly.

"Lovely," she said, her cheeks warm and flushed.

Paige walked with Felicia to a small trailer where the actress scrubbed off the heavy makeup and changed into a baggy sweatshirt and jeans. After tying a scarf around her head and pushing oversize sunglasses onto her nose, Felicia looked in the mirror and nodded in satisfaction. "Works every time," she said. "No one recognizes me when I'm done up like this. We'll have a fun afternoon like perfectly normal people. Did you bring your car?"

"No, Paul drove us over."

"I have a rented one, so we're all set. I hate taxis. I always feel like such a snob asking someone to take me around while I sit in the backseat. You pick the shops. We've got to find something gorgeous."

Felicia chattered nonstop as Paige gave directions to Fifth Avenue in Scottsdale and it was difficult for Paige to remember she was in the company of a world-famous movie star. In her sweatshirt and jeans Felicia appeared more like a housewife who had decided to escape from scrubbing the kitchen floor.

"Paul Martin is a doll," Felicia said as they glanced in the windows of the boutiques. "I suppose I should have waited to find out if he's involved with anyone before I pounced on him to take me to the party."

"He's footloose and fancy-free," Paige said.

"Oh, good. I'm hoping he'll make my stay here much more enjoyable. Paige, look at that dress! It would be perfect for you."

The creation in the window was a floor-length red velvet gown with a deep, plunging neckline. The skirt flared slightly in soft folds, and the material appeared lush and rich.

"It's rather . . . daring," Paige said doubtfully.

"Kellen will die on the spot," Felicia said, grabbing Paige by the arm. "Come on, let's see if they have your size."

The dress was heavenly. It fit Paige as though it had been custom-made. Twirling around to glimpse herself from every angle in the mirror, Paige felt like Cinderella about to go to the ball. She had never owned anything so elegant or quite so sexy. Felicia gushed profusely, declaring Paige to be an absolute vision of loveliness, and helped her select thin-strapped silver evening sandals with a matching clutch to complete the ensemble. With her purchases wrapped in tissue and carefully tucked in pretty blue boxes, Paige nearly floated out of the store, holding her precious treasures.

The afternoon flew by as the two women ate lunch in a quaint tearoom and then scoured the city for a gown for Felicia. They finally settled on a black satin dress that accentuated Felicia's ample bustline and showed off her thick mane of red hair to perfection. They were tired when Felicia dropped Paige off at the House of Martin, and each thanked the other for a delightful day.

Back in her flower-filled apartment, Paige took a leisurely bubble bath, then pulled on jeans and a nubby-knit red sweater. When Kellen arrived at nine, he looked exhausted. He apologized for the late hour, but explained they had run into difficulties in several technical areas of the picture and had spent the afternoon and evening in meetings.

"So," he said, pulling her close as she snuggled next to him on the sofa, "did you enjoy your glimpse of show biz?"

"I made such a fool of myself," she said, laughing, "but, yes, I had a wonderful time."

"I was very touched to think you were trying to protect me from that dude who wanted to snuff me out."

"I couldn't just stand there and let him shoot you!"

"I loved the whole bit. Did you and Felicia have fun?"

"Oh, yes. We found the most beautiful dresses. She's such a nice person, Kellen."

"That she is. Anyone else you're particularly fond of?"

"Paul is high on my list," she teased.

"And Kellen Davis?" he asked, placing nibbling kisses down the slender column of her throat. "Where does he fit in?"

Only in my heart and soul and mind, she thought, a wave of desire surging through her. "Would my bed do for now?" she asked, surprising herself with her boldness.

"Lady, I like the way you think," Kellen said, getting to his feet and offering her his hand.

Their lovemaking was quiet and tender, Kellen's fatigue causing him to roam slowly over Paige with his hands and lips, as if rejuvenating himself with the sweetness of her willing body and fragrant skin. She stroked him as she might a tired child, feeling his tense muscles relax under her soothing touch. Without speaking, he came to her at last, thrusting within her as she arched her back to receive the fullness that consumed her. They soared, higher and higher, until with echoing moans they exploded into a rapturous world known only to themselves. They drifted back in a delicious inertia, the night darkness of Kellen's thick hair glistening with perspiration as he pulled Paige close and sighed deeply.

"You're so tired," Paige said softly. "Go to sleep, Kellen."

"I have an early call. I don't want to wake you when I leave."

"I want you here, with me. It doesn't matter what time you have to get up. Please, Kellen, stay."

"Talked me into it."

"Good."

"Paige, I thought about you so much after you left

the set today. I was up to my neck in complications, but a part of my mind kept thinking that when it was over I could come to you and everything would be fine."

"And here I am." She trailed her fingertip down his chest.

"That's the point. You *are* here and I can't ever begin to tell you how much that means to me. You've become a part of me, an extension of my being. I've never felt this way before. I've made my work my life because it was all I had. Now I put you first and fit everything else in around the edges."

"Oh, Kellen . . ."

"Paige, it took me a while to figure out what was happening. But today when you flipped out because you thought I was going to be hurt, it all fell into place."

"I don't understand, Kellen. I embarrassed you in front of your colleagues and—"

"No. Your actions said, or rather screamed, that you care for me. Really care. I was bursting with pride. I was thinking, Hey, world, are you seeing this? This incredibly beautiful, wonderful lady is ready to go up against a man with a gun to protect me. I knew, Paige, that if things were reversed, I'd put my life on the line for you. I'd die before I'd let anything happen to you because you've—you've become my reason for being."

"You're going to make me cry."

"Paige, I've never said this to any woman before and doing it now scares the hell out of me. But I have to. I have to tell you."

"What is it, Kellen?"

"I love you. Paige, I love you with my whole heart. I guess that sounds corny, but I sincerely mean it. I love you."

A clamor of voices seemed to scream in Paige's

mind. He couldn't love her! He mustn't! By doing that he was sentencing himself to the same heartache and pain that she would suffer when their time together had ended. Why had he done this?

"Paige?" Kellen said, a deep frown creasing his brow as he felt her stiffen in his arms.

"I never dreamed you felt this way."

"I can sure tell you're not thrilled with my news-flash," he said tersely, sitting up on the edge of the bed.

"It just came as such a surprise."

"You forgot your line, Paige," he said, his jaw tight. "You're supposed to say 'I love you too, Kellen.' But I guess that only happens in the movies, huh?"

"Kellen, please—"

"If you don't love me, then what has all this been about?" he roared, tugging on his clothes. "You claim you're past using me to rid you of your dead husband's ghost. It was you and me. Together. God, we shared so much. We built a foundation that withstood the mistakes and let us continue on. I thought we had it all. Heaven help me, I love you, but the fact that you don't feel the same about me is more than I can handle. What tag do you put on it? Infatuation? Physical attraction?"

"No! Kellen, I—"

"Well?"

She couldn't tell him she loved him, she thought frantically. His anger would make him forget her. He'd be spared the agony of finally admitting their worlds were too far apart and the knowledge that there was no hope for a future together. When he left Phoenix, he might be bitter for a while, but at least he wouldn't agonize over a mutual love that wasn't meant to be. "I'm sorry, Kellen," she said softly, a sob catching in her throat.

A haunting pain swept through Kellen's eyes. His

face appeared suddenly drawn and pale as he finished buttoning his shirt with trembling hands. Then without a further word he turned and left the room, the sound of the front door closing reaching Paige's ears moments later.

She lay perfectly still, hands clenched in tight fists as she stared at the ceiling. Kellen was gone. Forever. An icy misery that seemed to freeze her inner soul covered her like a shroud. She had been the Good Samaritan, the martyr who had thrown herself to the wolves to shield her lover. It had been a grand, noble gesture, and it hurt with an indescribable pain. She knew deep within her that Kellen's pride and male ego would see him through this. He would rationalize her away, convince himself she had been an error in judgment, and he was well rid of her after all. Her refusal to declare her love would provide him with the tool he would need to exorcise her from his mind.

"Oh, Kellen," she said, her voice a hushed whisper, "I do love you. My love is so deep, it will give me the strength to do this, to walk away from you and never return. Good-bye, my Kellen."

Sobs racked her body and she cried for hours, her tears erasing the last of the lingering aroma of Kellen from her pillow. Toward dawn she slept, huddled in a ball like a frightened little girl who had been left alone in the darkness.

When she awoke, she felt exhausted, drained, and went through her morning routine automatically, not allowing herself to think or dwell on the events of the night before. Arriving at Kellen's, she unlocked the front door for Scott Howlett and his crew but did not go inside. She wasn't prepared to enter that house, not yet, and quickly told Scott she had pressing business before running down the steps and driving away.

She moaned inwardly the moment she saw Janet

when she entered the House of Martin. In the excitement of being on the movie set, both she and Paul had forgotten to get Kellen's autograph for the secretary.

"That's okay," Janet said when Paige apologized. "I can wait. After all, you see him every day. Boy, Mrs. Cunningham, my eyes nearly popped out of my head when I read the society column this morning. Mr. Martin is involved with Felicia Evans? Wow! That is something. I bet the four of you really have a super time when you're together. Of course, if it was me and I belonged to Kellen Davis, I sure wouldn't want to double-date. I'd rather—"

"Excuse me, Janet," Paige said, "but I must get to work."

"Oh. Sure thing."

"Is Mr. Martin in?"

"No."

Thank goodness for that much, Paige thought, going into her office and seating herself behind her desk. Paul knew her too well. He'd see in an instant that something was wrong.

Pulling some blank pieces of paper out of her desk, Paige stared at them for several minutes before picking up a colored pencil and beginning to sketch. During the drive back from Kellen's she had formulated a scheme in her mind that would make it possible to spend minimal time in Kellen's home. Her original plan had been to arrange the furniture and accessories once Scott had finished painting the walls and decide then if the room needed any additional items. Now, however, she would draw everything out on paper and make her final decision from that. It was not the most professional way to handle the job, but it was the best she could do emotionally under the circumstances.

"I'm off to lunch," Janet said much later, poking her head in the door.

"Is it that late? All right, Janet, I'll see you in an hour."

"I can bring you something back if you're staying in."

"Thanks, but I'm really not hungry."

"Okay. Bye."

Leaning back in her chair, Paige rocked her head back and forth in an attempt to loosen the muscles in her neck that ached from the hours spent bent over the intricate drawing. Getting up, she walked to the windows and glanced down at the busy Phoenix street. A sense of déjà vu swept over her as she remembered the last time she had stood there looking at the Christmas decorations and the Santa Claus on the corner, who was still ringing his trusty bell.

On that previous occasion she had been filled with the horrors of the past. Now, at last, Jerry was gone. But this Christmas? she thought. How was she going to survive it without Kellen? No, she refused to cry any more tears. She'd go over every detail of their shared moments, wrap them up like a gift, and present it to herself on Christmas morning. He'd given her back the joy of this season, and her last gesture of love would be to smile through that day. It would be the finishing touch of their relationship.

"Paige?" Paul said, startling her out of her reverie. "What in the hell is going on?"

"What do you mean?"

"I just had lunch with Felicia. She's very upset. She said Kellen came on the set this morning mad as hell about something. He chewed out everyone, and when Felicia asked him what was wrong, he told her to mind her own damn business. She's convinced there must be trouble between you and Kellen."

"I see," Paige said, turning back to the window.

"Paige, talk to me!"

"I can't, Paul, not now. I promised myself I wouldn't cry anymore. I'm too fragile to try and explain it all to you without falling apart. All I can say is that it's over between Kellen and me but please, don't press me. Later, when I've had some time, I'll share it with you."

"Dammit." Paul walked over to her and pulled her into his arms. "Why do you always have to be hurt? I don't know what happened to split you and Kellen, but whatever it is, I hate it. You deserve to be happy, Paige."

"Please don't pity me, Paul," she said, stepping out of his embrace and looking at him steadily. "I've had the most beautiful love imaginable. Some people never experience that. Kellen Davis touched my life and brought me such contentment. It was short, but so very sweet, and I'll cherish every moment."

"But—"

"I really need to finish these sketches," she said, walking to her desk and sitting down.

"Okay, I get the message that you want to be alone. Just remember I'm here if you need a friend."

"Thank you, Paul."

Paige arrived at Kellen's at five o'clock to lock up after Scott Howlett and was relieved to hear that the painting had been completed. Taking a deep breath, she squared her shoulders and entered the house, concentrating only on giving her usual final inspection to the job. She nodded in approval, thanked Scott for his excellent work, and quickly drove away.

At her apartment she stood inside the door and gazed at the multitude of floral bouquets. After changing into jeans and a sweater, she carried them one by one down the corridor, leaving them outside the doors of her neighbors, whom she had never met.

They'll think there really is a Santa Claus, she thought, laughing suddenly as she sank wearily onto the sofa. She was so tired. She'd had enough of this day. She was going to bed. Alone. Without Kellen.

"Stop it," she said aloud, getting to her feet. "Don't start feeling sorry for yourself."

The following days were a blur as Paige tied up loose ends on her much neglected accounts. Several of her clients seemed to treat her with a new sense of awe, viewing her now, she realized, as the woman Kellen Davis had chosen to be his lady during his stay in Phoenix. Several made reference to the movie star, obviously trying to wiggle some juicy tidbit out of her. Paige became very adept at sidestepping any reference to Kellen.

She had not returned to Kellen's house since the day she had inspected the painting. The sketches of the living room revealed an ominously bare corner, and she was mentally toying with what she should put in it, browsing through shops as time allowed.

Of Paul she had seen little. He'd stop in the doorway of her office and inquire sincerely if she was really all right. Once assured that she wasn't about to jump off the roof, he would hurry on his way. When Janet produced eight-by-ten autographed pictures of both Kellen and Felicia, Paige surmised that all of Paul's spare time was being spent with the beautiful red-haired actress.

Taking only small emotional steps at a time, Paige was now able to think of Kellen without immediately fighting back the tears she refused to shed. But always present was the dull ache in her heart for what might have been.

At last she found exactly what she needed to complete Kellen's living room: three hand-woven baskets in different shapes and sizes. She filled them with dried desert flowers and at a prearranged time met at Kellen's the two men she often hired to move furniture in newly decorated homes. They had the patience of saints and never complained if Paige had them lug sofas and chairs around a room over a dozen times until she was completely satisfied. She had no intention of lingering at Kellen's, however, and arrived with the sketch in her hand. Within a half hour the job was completed and the men left, wishing her a happy holiday.

Paige stood alone in the enormous room, her professional training causing her to scrutinize every inch of the expanse. Pleased with what she saw, she picked up her purse and removed the Christmas gift she had purchased for Timmy Winslow. She set it carefully on one of the gleaming end tables and, without looking back, walked out of the house for the last time. She would instruct Janet to mail Kellen the key with the final accounting. The job was finished. The relationship between Paige Cunningham, the decorator, and Kellen Davis, the client, was over.

On the morning of Kellen's Christmas party, Paige awoke feeling depressed. Still lying in bed, she envisioned the beautiful red velvet dress that was hanging in her closet and remembered the enjoyable afternoon she had spent with Felicia selecting the gown. Tonight Kellen's house would be aglow with lights and ringing with music. Laughter would dance through the multitude of rooms and a good time would be had by all.

"Hell's bells," Paige muttered, shuffling into the bathroom. "I just might jump off the roof after all. Cancel that. I'm too chicken."

The minute Paige arrived at the office, Janet jumped up waving a piece of paper. "Look at this, Mrs. Cunningham," the girl said. "Mr. Martin is closing the House of Martin at noon today and not opening again until January second. We all get vacations. With pay!"

"Let me see that," Paige said, quickly reading the memo addressed to all the staff. "Well, that's very generous of him."

"Personally," Janet said, lowering her voice to a whisper, "I think he's going off somewhere with Felicia Evans. I just bet that's what this is all about."

"Who knows?" Paige shrugged. Thanks a bunch, Paul, she thought as she headed for her office. All she needed right now was an overdose of extra hours on her hands with nothing to do.

An hour later Paige was deeply engrossed in studying a large sample book of material swatches that had arrived in the mail. Suddenly Janet burst into the office, her face flushed as she gasped for breath.

"Lord, Janet," Paige said, "are you ill?"

"He's here! He's here! Oh, my God, I can't believe it!"

"Janet, calm down. He who? What he is here? Or however that goes."

"Kellen Davis is standing in front of my desk at this very minute!"

"What?" Paige said, her eyes wide.

"He wants to see you but I said I had to check because you told me never to show anyone in unless they had an appointment but I'm sure that didn't include Kellen Davis but I thought—"

"Janet!"

"Am I babbling? I can't help it, Mrs. Cunningham. He's so gorgeous. Shall I show him in?"

"He's in," Kellen said from the doorway. "Thank you, Janet, you're a very efficient secretary."

"I am?" She blushed. "Well, uh, of course, I am. Yes. Well. Good-bye."

"Good-bye, Janet," Kellen said, flashing her a radiant smile as he closed the door behind her. "Hello, Paige," he said quietly, walking slowly toward the desk.

Dressed in jeans and a black sweater, he looked magnificent to Paige until she saw the tight line of his jaw and the coldness in his blue eyes. The word that came to her mind was *menacing*, and she clasped her hands together in her lap so Kellen couldn't see their trembling.

"I'm surprised to see you, Kellen," she said, hoping her voice sounded steady.

"I'm here on business," he said.

"Please, sit down. Is there some problem with the decorating I did for you?"

"No," he said, sitting in the chair opposite her and crossing his long legs. "The house is fine. Fantastic. I'm very pleased."

"Is there a question about the bill?" Oh, Kellen, say whatever it is and leave, she thought. She wanted to rush into his arms so badly. She loved him so much.

"No. Everything is in order. I've given my accountant instructions to pay it immediately."

"Then what—"

"I'm here to collect a personal debt. You owe me, Paige Cunningham," he said, his eyes locking onto hers.

"I don't understand."

Kellen pushed himself to his feet, placing his hands on the desk as he leaned forward. Paige flattened herself against her chair, a rush of panic enveloping her as she looked up at his stony expression.

"Then I'll explain it to you," he said, his voice low and rumbly. "When I met you, Paige, you had forgotten the meaning of Christmas and the joy this season brings. I helped you overcome your ghosts and freed you to once again take part in the holidays with a genuine smile. I wanted you to reclaim that kind of happiness, enjoy the festivities, feel young and carefree. You do remember, don't you, Paige?"

"Yes, of course, and I'm very grateful to you for—"

"You robbed me, Paige," Kellen suddenly roared, causing her to jump with fright. "You stole every bit of enthusiasm and anticipation I had for this Christmas. I have over two hundred people arriving at my house tonight for a party I no longer give a damn about!"

"Kellen, I—"

"You're going to give me my Christmas back, do you hear me? You're coming to that party and, by God, you'll smile and laugh and stay next to me the whole evening."

"That's crazy!" Paige yelled. "What's the point in pretending, playing a game?"

"That's how it's going to be. I'll face tomorrow when it gets here, but tonight, dammit, everyone, including me, will believe you're still my lady. You'll see to it that I have a Christmas I can look back on with fond memories."

"No, Kellen!"

"I'll send a car for you at nine. Be ready. Rest assured, Paige, if you don't show up, I'll come and get you."

"This is insane!"

"Nine o'clock," he growled, turning and striding from the room with long heavy steps.

"My God," Paige whispered, covering her face with her hands. "Why is he doing this to me? Why?"

Hours later Paige's nerves were so jangled, she was pacing her living room with sharp, staccato movements. She had given up trying to work at the office and after wishing Janet, who was still starry-eyed from Kellen's visit, a merry Christmas, drove home only to find she was totally unable to relax.

She'd hide, she thought frantically. She'd go to a

movie. She'd go to a bar. She'd go out of her mind if she spent an entire evening close to Kellen. Her love for him would show in her eyes, and he'd know.

Sinking onto the sofa, she rested her elbows on her knees and cupped her chin in her hands. Maybe, just maybe, she could pull it off. Kellen had demanded that she perform for him, play the part of his devoted lover. Anything that he might construe from her expressions or actions she could claim to be an excellent job of acting. She would simply live the true role of Paige Cunningham being deeply in love with Kellen Davis, and he'd never know she wasn't faking. It would work. It had to! For some reason beyond her comprehension Kellen was determined to have his Christmas with her by his side, and she would be there, savoring each moment, storing it away for the cold, lonely nights ahead. They would have their Christmas after all, if only in their separate private fantasies.

In a burst of energy Paige dashed into the bedroom and stripped off her clothes. She would be beautiful tonight, like Cinderella, and as in the fairy tale, when the clock struck twelve, it would be over. Only this time Prince Charming wouldn't comb the countryside looking for his princess. Kellen Davis would simply walk away.

Promptly at nine o'clock a knock sounded at Paige's door. She shivered slightly, then lifting her chin to a determined tilt, answered the summons to find a uniformed man, who tipped his cap, standing before her. Minutes later she was seated in the backseat of a long, luxurious limousine, speeding through the surging traffic. The huge automobile seemed to gobble up the miles, and the chauffeur soon turned into the familiar circular drive leading to Kellen's house. The entire area was filled with cars, and lights were shining in many of the windows of the big house.

Leaving the comforting warmth of the vehicle, Paige pulled her shawl closer around her shoulders and walked slowly up the steps to the front door.

As she raised her hand to knock, the wooden panel opened revealing Kellen, who was dressed in a black suit and tie with a formal ruffled white shirt.

"Good evening, Paige," he said quietly. "I've been waiting for you."

"Kellen." She nodded and walked past him into the entryway.

Decorative screens had been placed across the tiled expanse to keep the chill off the people at the end of the hall, who were dancing to the music provided by a six-piece band. With Kellen's hand resting lightly on her elbow she walked into the living room, where an enormous Christmas tree was twinkling in magnificent splendor against the far wall. The guests were dressed in their finery, talking and laughing in small groups as uniformed waiters moved among them, carrying trays of drinks and food.

"Let me have your shawl and purse," Kellen said. He handed them to an unencumbered waiter. "You look beautiful, Paige, like a Christmas doll."

"Thank you. Felicia picked out my dress."

"I haven't really greeted you properly, have I?" Kellen said, his voice low and husky.

Oh, no, he was going to kiss her, she thought wildly.

And he did.

Kellen kissed her with such tenderness, she nearly burst into tears. He looked deep into her eyes when he at last lifted his head, and she almost sobbed aloud at the sadness she saw reflected in his own eyes.

He was a dirty, rotten player, she decided, picking an imaginary thread off her dress while she struggled to regain her composure.

For the next hour Kellen introduced Paige to everyone in the place. Paul and Felicia appeared surprised to see her there, but before they could comment, Kellen whisked her on to the next group. The silly part about the whole ordeal was that Kellen insisted that each member of his crew pull out pictures of children, wives, girlfriends, or whatever seemed to be dear to their hearts. After gushing over a photograph of a cocker spaniel, Paige pleaded for something to drink.

"Of course, darling," Kellen said, circling her shoulders with his arm. "Forgive me for not thinking of it sooner."

"I hope you're not going to test me on all those people's names," she said, sipping champagne from a crystal glass.

"No," Kellen said, a smile tugging at the corners of his mouth, "that wasn't the purpose of that number."

"Oh?"

"I thought you might be interested in seeing that all these supposedly decadent Hollywood people are in actuality very devoted to their families. They're simply working in areas where they have talent, and at night they go home to the ones they love. None of us, including me, are from a different planet. We're just earning a living doing whatever it is we do best."

"But the star, the big important man, can never turn it off, can he, Kellen? It follows him wherever he goes, robs him of his privacy, leaves no room for anything or anyone."

"That's not true, Paige. Every profession has some kind of cross to bear. Doctors are asked for free medical advice at cocktail parties. Parents bug teachers in restaurants, wanting to know why their kid flunked out."

"I suppose that's true, but—"

"The whole key to survival is a man's priorities. He

has to decide when he's had enough giving of his very soul, and then back off to have space to breathe. The doctor and teacher simply say, 'Call me in the morning.' The sex symbol, the superstar, tells the whole world he's chosen one woman to share his life. The people, his fans, can decide for themselves if they'll accept who he's now become. Would you like to dance?"

"I— yes. Fine," Paige said, her mind whirling from the impact of Kellen's words. Was he saying he would actually publicly declare his love for her at the risk of destroying the image he had worked so many years to build? Or was she reading between the lines, changing chitchat into meaningful statements she wanted, needed to hear? But if it was true, if he really meant—

"Paige, my dear child," Timmy said, seeming to pop out of the woodwork, "you look ravishing. Thank you so much for the lovely gift. It was so thoughtful of you to remember me."

"You're welcome, Timmy." She smiled warmly at him.

"Kellen," Timmy said, "I hate to talk business at this marvelous party, but I've had a call from Pat. She's decided not to return from her maternity leave. When we go back to the studio in January, we have no set designer, my boy."

"Well, damn," Kellen said, frowning.

"You know, Paige," Timmy said, "with what I've seen you do with this castle in such a short time, you'd be a splendid replacement for Pat. Of course, we need someone right away. I imagine you have months of work already commissioned."

"Not really," she said. "All my accounts had Christmas deadlines and then, out of the blue, Paul closed the House of Martin until after the holidays."

"You don't say," Timmy said.

"But that doesn't mean I'd even consider—"

"Excuse us, Timmy," Kellen interrupted. "Paige and I were about to dance."

"Enjoy," Timmy said, beaming as Kellen pulled Paige away.

The chandelier in the entryway had been dimmed to cast a soft luminosity over the area, and several couples were swaying to dreamy music. Kellen drew Paige into his arms, and she molded herself to his massive frame. He felt good. And smelled good. And had tasted so good when he had kissed her. This was where she belonged, she told herself, safely tucked away in the strong embrace of the man she loved. For a few minutes she allowed herself the luxury of drinking in the feel of Kellen's body, remembering every beautiful inch of it. The night was so wonderful, and enchanting, and . . . strange, she thought, stumbling slightly only to have Kellen pull her closer to his chest.

Suddenly her eyes widened as the jumbled pieces in her mind fell together like a jigsaw puzzle. Stopping abruptly, she looked up at Kellen. "I want to talk to you!" she said firmly.

"Go ahead."

"Not here. Privately."

"Come into my den."

"Just don't think I'm an unsuspecting fly, bub," she said. She marched past him and threw him a stormy look over her shoulder that silenced his throaty chuckle.

"That spider dude had a parlor, not a den," he said.

"Whatever," she muttered, walking into the empty room that was brightly lit by a twinkling chandelier that hung from the ceiling. "All right, Kellen," she said, turning to face him after he'd closed the door, "something smells fishy."

"Must be the paint."

"Don't get cute! I want to know what's going on!"

"To what are you referring?" he asked, an innocent look on his face. Uh-oh, he thought. She had figured it out.

"I just realized that every one of those men who shoved pictures of their families, dogs, and pet frogs under my nose took those photographs out of their pockets. Not wallets, Kellen. Maybe one or two are so devoted that they carry them around loose even in a tuxedo, but thirty or forty guys? No way! Someone told them to be prepared to play Show-and-Tell."

"I'll be darned," Kellen said, stroking his chin thoughtfully.

"And," she said, planting her hands on her slender hips, "isn't it a remarkable coincidence that your set designer quit right at the time that Paul closed down for the holidays, which he has never done before?"

He shrugged. "Beats me."

"Kellen Davis, you conned me! You set me up! That performance of yours in my office was an act, a ploy to get me out here to witness whatever it is you're staging! It's truth time, Kellen."

"Yes, it is," he said softly, crossing the room to her and resting his hands on her shoulders. "You're right about everything. I did put on a show in your office, but it worked because you came."

"You bum!"

"And I carefully coached my crew to have those pictures ready to whip out. I've known for a week that Pat wasn't coming back, but Timmy played his part very well. Paul was in on it, too, and agreed to close the House of Martin for now so you'd be free."

"But why?"

"Paige, I was desperate. I had to try something, anything, to win you back. I've had a lot of time to think since I last saw you because I haven't slept worth a damn. It suddenly became very clear to me, Paige."

"It did?"

"You are in love with me." Dear God, he thought, let him be right. She had to love him! He couldn't go on without her.

"What?"

"I know you, Paige, almost as well as I know myself. You gave yourself to me totally, completely. Not just when we made love, but by sharing your inner secrets, hopes, and fears. You allowed me to tear down that protective wall you were hiding behind because you trusted and believed in me. You forgave me when I hurt you and let me show you how to laugh again. That all adds up to love, Paige."

"Kellen . . ." she started, tears blinding her vision.

"But you wouldn't tell me how you felt. You were protecting me from what you thought was an impossible dream. You were convinced we had no future together because of the world I live in and the demands it makes on me. That's why I had to get you to this party. I wanted to show you that these people are decent human beings with normal lives. I meant it when I said I would tell the whole universe that I love only you and let the chips fall where they may."

"Kellen . . ." she tried again.

"Paige, we can have it all, don't you see? We'll be together on the movie sets because you'll be the set designer. Between films we can live here and make beautiful love through the lazy days and nights. I need you, Paige, to celebrate every Christmas with me for the rest of my life. Say you love me. Please, Paige, let me hear the words."

"Oh, Kellen." She began to sob as tears ran unchecked down her cheeks. "I do! I love you so much, I can hardly bear it. I didn't want you to be hurt, be plagued by ghosts as I had been. I thought if you were angry, you'd forget me sooner and . . . I don't know how you read my mind, but I'm so grateful you did. I love you and I want to be with you always."

"Marry me, Paige. Stand by my side and promise you'll never leave me again."

"Yes! Yes! I'll marry you!"

"Thank God." He pulled her into his arms and kissed her deeply, leaving her trembling and bursting with desire. "Just one other thing," he said finally, taking a ragged breath. "Do you think when you finish decorating this house, you could make one of the bedrooms a nursery? That is, I mean, if you think you'd—"

"I want to have your baby, Kellen. I'll put together the prettiest room imaginable. It will be perfect, the finishing touch."

"Thank you, my love. Paige, there are two hundred people standing outside that door, holding their breath and waiting to see if my diabolical plan worked. Let's go tell them the good news."

"All right." She smiled joyfully and brushed the tears off her cheeks.

"I love you, Paige Cunningham."

"Merry, *merry* Christmas, Kellen Davis," she whispered.

EDITOR'S CORNER

Did you ever harbor a secret desire to be able to pick a lock with a hairpin? crack a safe? outwit a cunning mastermind? I sure have—especially when my front door key sticks in the lock . . . when I can't even wrench open the cabinet in the tool shed . . . uh, and about that cunning mastermind, I have to confess we've been having a bit of trouble at home convincing our puppy that she isn't boss of the house!

Well, if you too have fantasized about having some of the skills of a female 007, you are going to be mad about Kay Hooper's Troy Bennett in **ILLEGAL POSSESSION,** LOVESWEPT #83. You know Kay's wonderful romances so, even if you aren't a fan of derring-do traits in your heroines, I predict that still you'll love this entrancing book. Troy relishes the thrills in her unusual line of work while avoiding anything even remotely dangerous in matters of the heart. Then she encounters the sexy, powerful, and upstanding, almost self-righteous Dallas Cameron. Blinking red lights . . . emotional danger for Troy and trouble for the scrupulous Dallas. But they can't resist one another! Just how these two delightfully different people mellow and change to accommodate each other provides a love story you won't soon forget!

BJ James's romance next month, **A STRANGER CALLED ADAM,** LOVESWEPT #84, is breathtakingly dramatic from first until last. An aura of mystery pervades Shadow Mountain and touches all who live beneath it. And no one is more touched by that mystery than Tracy Walker. One of the few who dares to challenge the mountain, who even lives on it, Tracy has a fascinating past and a challenging future . . .

(continued)

especially after she has rescued the daughter of Adam Grayson. Adam instantly recognizes Tracy from long ago and almost as quickly is captivated by her. But Shadow Mountain, like a living, breathing creature, looms between them—representing all that separates these two loving people from happiness together. BJ's love story, shimmering with passionate intensity, is indeed a memorable read.

I must say that the day Joan Elliott Pickart's first manuscript (unsolicited and I believe, addressed simply "Dear Editor") arrived in this office was a lucky day for all of us who love romance of humor, passion, and touching emotion. Nowhere will you find those qualities more evident tha in Joan's **ALL THE TOMORROWS,** LOVESWEPT #85. The first meeting between Dr. Sheridan Todd and Mr. David Cavelli is unusual, to put it mildly. The story swerves from the zany to a deeply touching account of the growing love and passion between Sheridan and David, especially as he tries to help her adopt the deaf child she cherishes and longs to mother. His intervention on her behalf in legal proceedings boomerangs and temporary custody of four-year-old Dominic is awarded to David. This most sensitive, loving man has only one flaw: a phobia about marriage. You'll be holding your breath between chuckles as you experience the delightful resolution of **ALL THE TOMORROWS**.

Now, rounding out this wonderful quartet of romance novels is Iris Johansen's **BLUE VELVET,** LOVESWEPT #86. If you guessed that Iris was going to give you Beau Lantry's love story, you were right on target! We rediscover Beau in a somewhat sleazy bar in a port town on a Caribbean Island. (Don't worry! Beau still only sips ginger ale!) His yacht is moored at the dock and he's out on the town for the evening. But any plans he might have been forming for the night come to a screeching end when Kate Gilbert enters the bar. Courage and heart are qualities Kate has in abundance; being sensible and calculating the consequences of acts are qualities she has in rather short supply! Beau to the rescue as a modern day knight on a white yacht, though Kate hardly sees herself as a damsel in distress. More often it's poor Beau who finds himself in distress as she embroils them in one hair-raising episode after another. For example, just imagine how drug runners respond when Kate destroys their cache of more than a million dollars' worth of cocaine . . . not to mention the reaction of corrupt cops when she sends two of their number off for a short nap with wine lightly laced with sleeping tablets. And through it all—even during high-speed chases at sea—the incredibly innocent and ridiculously brave Kate is capturing Beau's heart . . . just as she will yours. **BLUE VELVET** is one of Iris's most charming and madcap romps. Enjoy!

As always, thanks for your warm letters. We love hearing from you. With every good wish,

Sincerely,

Carolyn Nichols

Carolyn Nichols
Editor
LOVESWEPT
Bantam Books, Inc.
666 Fifth Avenue
New York, NY 10103

P.S. In case you missed the on sale date last month of Sandra Brown's marvelous historical, **SUNSET EMBRACE,** do remember to ask your bookseller for it when you go in to get this month's LOVESWEPTS!

A special excerpt of
the remarkable new novel
by the author of
A Many-Splendoured Thing and Till Morning Comes

The Enchantress

---

by Han Suyin

Dear Reader:

I'm delighted to announce the upcoming publication of Han Suyin's most recent novel, THE ENCHANTRESS, *an unforgettable tale of rich romance and intrigue set in Switzerland, China, and Thailand in the eighteenth century. It's a remarkable book, a sumptuous feast of the sights and sounds of a time gone by. And it's a story that only Han Suyin, whose life has spanned East and West, could tell.*

Enter a hidden world. Travel with Han Suyin to the eighteenth century, a time when the distinctions between magic, science, and the mystical spirits were far less clear than in our modern age. Meet adventurous Colin and his lovely twin sister Bea, whose Celtic ancestry has given them the Gift—the ability to hear each other's unspoken thoughts, especially in times of danger.

Sail with them to distant China, where Colin is called upon to repair the Emperor's magnificent clocks. On the way, see the city of Marseilles, sparkling between sun and water. Feel the caress of the wind at dawn. Breathe the perfumed scent of sandalwood and jasmine. And then, at journey's end, look in wonder at the glistening golden spires of Ayuthia as Colin and Bea enter the radiant city. Here, in splendor beyond their imagining, brother and sister will find greater love than each has ever known—and endure greater loss before Fate reveals what awaits them.

A bestselling author who's as charming as the stories she so skillfully tells, Han Suyin researches her books in China, the land of her birth, Switzerland, and India. THE ENCHANTRESS is sure to delight her millions of already devoted readers as well as win the hearts of new ones.

With the whisper of a delicate brush on silk paper, Han Suyin brings you into Ayuthia, the Enchantress, a world you will never forget.

With warm regards,

Tessa Rapoport
Senior Editor

Colin and Bea still tell the story of THE ENCHANTRESS in alternating voices, Bea's in italics. In this excerpt, they have reached Ayuthia. Colin (called Keran here) is about to wrestle with Chiprasong for the love of Jit, a woman whose name Colin does not yet know but who has won his heart. Prince Udorn, Colin's loyal friend, is the man Bea will marry, although she does not love him. Join them now as they begin their new life.

THE MATCHES WERE TO be held on the small plain of Bang Paket across the river, not far from the French settlement and its square-towered stone church of Saint Joseph. A large, happy crowd milled round the flat tamped field. The boxers and Krabi-Krabong swordsmen were ready. Chiprasong was already there, in a plain *pannung* or loincloth, his skin glistening with sandalwood oil. I think he wanted to be popular, to be known to the people as a simple man, perhaps to emulate the regretted King Boromakot, who often went among his people, clad as a commoner. Udorn and I sat down among the crowd, and the boxing began.

It was then, looking up, that I saw her, on the terrace of one of the stilt houses that lined one side of the field. She was with two older women, their hair shorn, and in black. She had turned her head to speak to one of them, and then she was looking at the crowd, as if looking for someone, and she saw me. I stared until I remembered that this meant scorn, and lowered my head, bringing it back to the boxers. Chiprasong had lifted his leg high to knock his opponent to the ground, but the latter, a limber young man and a fraction swifter, took a flying leap to bring Chiprasong to the ground. But Chiprasong stepped sideways and the young man missed.

I looked again, quickly glancing up. She was no longer on the terrace, and my heart began to pound wildly, as if I had lost an immense treasure. Oh let me see her but once again, oh let me see her . . . and then I did see her, she was on the outer edge of the circling crowd just opposite me and she was looking at me.

I did not know that I was in love then; only that the earth had changed under me, that my mind was wiped clean of everything else. Her face, her shoulders, the smallness and perfection of her. In a land where so many women were loveliness incarnate, it seemed to me that no one else but she alone was beautiful, truly so. Was she noble, was she a commoner? She wore the day's color, green for Wednesday, the *jongkra-bane* and top-tied halter as women at work did to keep their hands and legs free.

How could I approach her?

Udorn was bending over me. "Keran, Keran, are you dreaming? Chiprasong would like to have a round with you."

The sun was westering, its pink glow filled the sky, rose of a pearl. It touched her hair, her mouth. She wore a pink hibiscus in her hair.

Chiprasong strode up to me, assumed a boxing

stance, calling out something that made the crowd laugh. I felt hot all over.

"You cannot refuse; this is a friendly match. Better let him win quickly, so you will not be hurt." Udorn's voice was a little anxious. He replied gaily, however, and I knew that he was trying to make the crowd laugh at something else.

But the crowd really wanted some clowning now, to finish the day. Perhaps to see Chiprasong knock down a *farang*. There would be no dishonor in losing to the Tiger man, Prince Chiprasong.

No dishonor. Except that she was there. I could not be made a mockery of. I could not let Chiprasong beat me. She would see that I was lame when I stood up to fight. . . .

"The *farang* way, of course," he shouted.

As before any match, there was a short invocation, a gathering of the forces of the spirit and body, and then Chiprasong danced towards me, light on his feet, his knotted fists beautiful, almost caressing the air. He meant, I knew, to knock me down a few times, in as ridiculous a posture as possible, to draw laughter. He was grinning in a friendly manner. I hated him.

Watch his feet. He always feints with his right fist, kicks by wheeling his left foot. His big toe is lethal.

He came, lunging a deft right, a quick left, but I had already turned, letting his punch slide on my raised shoulder, and with my club foot hooked his ankle, while he was carried forwards by the momentum of his blow, and I whirled away from the impact of his body.

He stumbled but caught himself, and from a half-bent position swung once again towards my belly; but I had turned round on myself, and I was now behind him while he went forwards and fell on his back as I slammed his left arm backwards. . . .

He reeled and I seized his drooping wrist, twisting it hard and twisting him with it. Then with my good leg as a solid pillar I used my club foot to kick the back of the other knee. He fell then, and as he fell I chopped him in the neck with my free hand, a murderous blow.

He would not be up again for a while. I had tried to kill him. I had forgotten what Traveler had said: "Only self-defense, not to kill . . ."

She had seen that I was lame.

Udorn was handing me my tunic and my shoes, wiping the sweat off me. He was beaming, for I had won. "I did not know that you possessed the mastery of Zen," he said. "You keep secret many a thing, Keran."

I put on my cloth shoes, the one with a solid inner sole higher than the other first.

Men and women were pressing around me with joined hands, girls garlanding me with flowers. And she was there, smiling up at me; softly, shyly, her hands placed a garland round my neck.

The drums began. Double-headed *Tapone*, *Song-Na*, *Klong-Thad*, all the tunes of the Thai people, with their recall of hooves in the forest, of echoing tiger roar. Calling to the feast. The people of three villages had gathered, they squatted on palm leaves or on the ground. Men in black went about with pitchers of palm wine, carried vats of steaming food.

. . . Such a feast. Men coming to salute me, to ask me where I had learnt my fighting.

"Truly, tonight you are the *wang*, king of the feast," Udorn said exultingly.

Two women fanned me zealously throughout my eating, and on rattan trays in front of me were laid many bowls. I drank and ate, drank the hot palm wine. And then the dancing began.

The musicians arranged themselves in a circle, and

the drums now went sweet, precise and soft, like the pulse of night, like the beat of blood, a night so soft it was almost painful to be alive, to know that such nights are not given forever. The men rose to dance, and also the women, and she was there too, in the ranks of the women, until the thickening press of dancers hid her from my sight.

Drums. The night throbbed with them, and with the sound of the *pinai* flutes rising like nightingales, throaty and shrill and calling to the forest to listen.

Dancing—long weaving files of men, and across from them on the other side of the field, the women almost immobile save for the slow, ritual movement of the arms, the hands, the necks; meditative, weaving the spell of the enchanted night. Offering praise to the Lords of the Spirit for the goodness of the evening, the feast, the dance. . . .

And because of the palm wine emboldening me I made my way through the ranks of women until I found her, and folded my hands and bowed my head in front of her. We danced, five feet away from each other. She did not look at me, nor I at her; I kept my eyes down. Only my hands, my arms, said: I love you, I love you. The world has suddenly become a rainbow, become fragrant, delectable, because of you. Oh let me but love you, my hands said, weaving the air.

"Her name is Jit," Udorn told me when we were back in our *polun*, the rowers calling out the strokes. We were through the *Nei Kai*, the Chinese gate, which could always be opened, even at night.

"I shall die, Udorn, if I can't have her," I said. "Not my body, but something within me will die."

"Ah, the thunder and lightning of love is worse than any typhoon," Udorn said. "She is the daughter of a small official; she has Chinese blood in her, as well as Thai."

"I love her. That is all."

"Let me arrange it. You are not secretive, Keran. Everyone could see you were in love. Even Chiprasong saw it. He recovered from his faint and he was watching. I think he is angry because you shamed him. But now he should understand that it was because of love. You could not lose in front of her."

The rowers' oar blades whisked the water, pulling smoothly, beating time. Time, in slow oar beats, in slow heartbeats. Time had brought me here. I heard the croaking of the night frogs delighting in the watery night.

"Udorn, if she but come to me, I shall be the most blessed of men."

* * *

Anno Domini 1763–1764

I married Udorn at an auspicious hour in January of 1763. The ceremonies lasted three days: I changed my clothes twenty-one times, each time with a new set of jewels. Abdul Reza's generosity was unstinted; Udorn covered me with gifts. I now had five large chests of China lacquer with hinges and locks of pure gold, filled with jewelry and gold-threaded garments. And salvers and vases and boxes of gold, silver, enamel, ivory, and mother-of-pearl, enough to fill seven large cupboards.

Udorn is handsome. He has proved himself skilled and courteous as a lover. Since I do not love him I can all the more appreciate the pleasure he gives me. I keep intact the weather of my soul, and move towards my own freedom, undeterred, sovereign.

I think of the strong and bitter woman sitting in the Forbidden City of Peking: the Mother, Empress Dowager, who killed her son's love because she would not let him betray the Empire.

Perhaps she sometimes thinks of me.

Colin. Between my brother and me is a bond we must both maintain and resist. We have to shut our minds away from each other, since now we both have lovers; and we shall have to live with this interdiction all our lives. Perhaps others do, who bury deep within themselves their lust and hunger for a sister, a mother, to be more than sister or mother. With my brother and me it is a shallow grave, in which part of ourselves must lie forever.

Colin's love is a maiden shy and gentle, whose uncomplicated mind, like a rose, emits a wordless happiness. Whose body is slight, pliant, beautiful. She sees a bird and thinks: This is a bird. She goes no further, but to her the bird is all delight, marvel, joy. She will never grow weary of everyday small miracles. She has neither ambition nor malice. She wants only to serve Colin, to love him. This is her destiny.

Colin and I now speak words to each other, engage in philosophical discussions. He argues that time is a function of the universe; and that Newton has proved that time goes on, even if no one is there to make clocks, to measure time. I say that time shrinks or stretches according to the grip of our souls and the desire of our bodies. "Then you don't believe in my watches." Colin grins, looking young and boyish because he is happy.

In Newton's world are no spirits of tree and fire and enchanted forest. But here in Ayuthia are spirits everywhere, potent and powerful.

"Colin, the android you are thinking of making, he must be a king. He must have a king's face."

"The King?"

"Not Ekatat. Someone else. As yet I do not see his face. When I do, I shall make the face for you."

On the tenth day after our wedding I tell Udorn to bring

back his other wives. "They will grieve without you. Your heart is mine, so I am not jealous."

Udorn is delighted. A nobleman with only one wife is a pitiful thing in Ayuthia. Three of them are back; their speech the twitter of sparrows, their manners charming. "Three is enough," I say, and Udorn laughs, and calls me an enchantress, the queen of his heart.

The Gift is strong within me here, for Ayuthia is both dream and reality, fusion of everything contradictory, diverse, wayward, mutable.

"There will be war again, Udorn. The Burmese will come again."

"I know it, most beloved." He sighs. He and his cousin Phya *Cham are anxious and so is the* Kalahom, *for the ramparts of Ayuthia are in a poor state. Its many forts need repairs. There are no cannon balls for the cannon installed by the Portuguese under King Boromakot, Ekatat's father, some twenty years ago. Ekatat refuses to release the cannon and ammunition stored in the royal armory to strengthen the defense forts. The muskets of the palace guards have not been fired in many years.*

King Ekatat is besotted with shamans and exorcists who feed him philters, love potions, and quicksilver to make him invisible and invincible, so that, it is said, his teeth are beginning to drop away.

Udorn sighs. And nothing is done.

I go to see Abdul Reza in his house in the Muslim quarter with my retinue of maids and women fighters, Amazons trained to protect other women. I order them to withdraw. "I have important matters to talk over with Prince Reza." Now they know that I can do all I want—I am not fettered as other women are—and they leave me alone.

Abdul Reza sits, dignified, tormented. A man. A man with the smell and savor of a man. He reminds me of the

Chinese Emperor Tsienlung. He is the same age, with a body seasoned and inured with living and many women. I feel the stir of lust in me.

"I am yours, Lord Reza, if you so wish. For now I am no longer your ward, and I can choose the men I wish to make love with." His lips go pale. He moistens them.

"Lady, I cannot cheat."

"Udorn does not own me. I own myself."

His hands grip the small knife he wears always at his belt.

"You are wicked, immoral," he says, in a measured voice. "You play with people . . . you are cruel, Lady Bea."

"Wicked, cruel, immoral? Because I please myself, as a man pleases himself with women?"

A week later, he becomes mine, and pleasures me greatly, for he has a wonderful body, spare, undiminished by age; passion and anger make him fierce, indefatigable.

"You have taken my manhood from me," he says afterwards.

"But we shall always remember this hour," I reply. "For we were truthful with each other, were we not?"